Peace Be with You

by

Dewitt Jones, Ed.D

Special Thanks and Dedication

Special thanks to my wife Joanna for her support on this project, as well as the many friends who read it before it was ready to publish and gave helpful feedback. Dr. Jeanette McGreevy edited the manuscript and provided excellent creative input on the project.

I dedicate this book to Mary Agnus Barber, one of my high school teachers at Glenbrook North High School in Northbrook, Illinois. I would not have graduated from high school, gone to college, and eventually received a doctorate if she hadn't mentored me.

Kindle Direct Publishing – 2019

Revised - 2021

Preface

"Paris is under attack—this time multiple sites citywide."

Cold words whispered hoarsely into President Sutton's left ear (the good one) while the 7:29 morning mist calmly spread over the shaved and shaved White House lawn again. As Secretary of State Clark marched his fastidiously shined Oxfords from Oval Office to the situation room for Cabinet Briefing, the President immediately thought him an uptight, delusional, and inept odd duck—the harbinger of fallacy news, alternative truths, and overly-glistened lies. She had appointed him; now, she wanted him gone.

The President mused, "Last week, Prime Minister Girard Astor scorched the international press for questioning his word that he had plenty of screens and watchdogs in place to prevent terrorist attacks. His media crucifixion for that, I bet, well underway. What the hell?"

Snapping her eyes with a long-ago flash memory of Paris Chanel, Paris baguettes, Paris perspiration, and Paris pee, President Sutton wondered if they were gone—those olio odors replaced by gun exhaust, bomb smolder, and high-speed-fear vomit? The President stood, arms braced on the situation room table, an oaken octopus squirting decades of governing distress, as Clark's briefing ensued, "Thank you, everyone, for coming." President Sutton noted his then dramatic pause for I-am-in-the-know; you-are-not effect. "Terrorists used assault rifles, hand grenades, and suicide vests—the worst attack on France since WWII. Multiple-site strikes planned and executed with military precision: over 100 deaths and 540+ injured. DGSE will be in direct contact with the US Homeland Security Department to determine why the terrorist intentions were not previously detected. The splinter group XTREM involvement suspected." Sutton nodded executive approval in public acknowledgment of Clark's skillfully grim report. Her political enemies loved this power-grubbing windbag, and he, she suspected, secretly returned the affection.

By 8:15 am, the morning mist had soured into a deep White House fog, steaming with angry eyes to the east . . . from where the carnage and chaos might come . . . might arrive on American shores . . . might be in multiple sites in the same city . . . *like Paris.*

President Sutton squinted hard now, her eyes straining to find some save-the-day assurance in Clark's face as they moved away from the Situation Room, suppressing her thoughts that the *carnage deliverers were already here . . . God, where is Stan?*

"Stanley, stop squirming. I told you to leave that girl alone." He could not and had not for many months now.

Stanley Pace had been attending mass with his mother since, like forever. Clean shirt, straight back, and mouth shut. His mother, Beulah Pace, thrived on the almighty ritual, the sameness, and the power; his father, Alden Pace, PhD., not so much. So the eight-times-a-month routine was a mother/son-only affair. Stanley could rely on Mass and Rosary like the certainty of clean breezes off San Francisco Bay and the leather/tobacco smell of his dad's University of Berkley briefcase. While Stanley loved his mother, however, the obedience required to Pope, Bishop, and Mother Mary strained his 10-year-old adventurous sensibilities. He often tried and prevailed as a religious supplicant, but as often as not, fell into the potboiler of Rhoda sin—despite the eight-times-a-month excursions to row twelve.

In Stan's young mind, tormenting Rhoda Roberts at twice-weekly mass gave him a self-imposed divinity of power. Upon pretense of heeding his mother's 15th warning with a firm pinch of his shoulder, Stanley plotted his next disembowelment of the Catholic-obedient Rhoda. "It's easy to make that ugly girl's rosary beads twist in the wind," he thought to himself. "Just stick out my tongue, pull on those stupid pigtails, call her witch face, or pretend to be nice and then slug her in the gut." That dumb, ugly girl just sat there. Easy Peasy.

"Stanley, if that girl makes you pay someday, you'll get what you deserve. God will see to it." Unfazed, Stanley pulled out his Rosary beads and figured that he had 95 more acts of mayhem to pull on Rhoda. This was a great game. He would quit after he tallied the last bead on the 108-bead ledger. "God, I hope it happens on a GLORIUS Sunday." *It may have if only he could remember . . .*

Dr. Stan Pace, forty years later and the weary Director of the Center for Disease Control, sat in St. Mary's mass in another row twelve on the opposite coast when President Sutton received the Paris news. Mass was well underway when Stan, having long-forgotten his bead-torment-scheme over that girl from St. Mary's long ago—what was her name? Rhonda? Ronnie? Oh, yes . . . RHODA watched a young smart-ass punk on his right throw a slimy spit-wad at his female victim in row ten.

Dr. Pace grimaced and prayed, "Hope you get yours, kid. God will see to it." While the rumple-shirted gremlin continued his torment during the Pontifical Incense ("Breathe it in, kid—you might be saved."), he wondered what Carol was up to. He had not seen her in several months, and he missed her voice, her face, and her body. Theirs was a dangerous game.

Chapter 1 - Vatican City

Vatican City reeked of overzealous supplicant piety and penniless mendicants in the months following the Pope's controversial ordination. Heat-waved courtyard cobblestones taunted the wealthiest papal donors with "walk-on-me-to-glory" promises. The sanctimonious entitled could ascend the Vatican steps first-in-line to relish in the papal blessing with enough coin. *Twenty grand—good. Fifty grand—better. One million—edifice status.* The constant camera-shuffling, shirt-tugging, adoring horde. *How much longer?* Doesn't matter. *Will he talk to us?* Doesn't matter. From the safety of the Holy See, Cardinal Lenza tired of suffering the daily spectacle from his balcony above the fray, his black Simar stiff with formality and self-importance, each crease a triumphant perfection of order and entitlement above the spiritual offenders below. Supplicant anticipation dulled the day again. The Cardinal could have been disinfectant to their sorry souls, but they were not his to cleanse. He had lost the big war to Papal glory, but he had every intention of winning the battle just ahead.

He smelled a new subtle power wafting in the Holy See air today, a fragrance for which he had waited too long. As the Cardinal darted his envious eyes to and fro on the daily parade of suits, sandals, and corporate crawlers sweat-shuffling to his Holiness, not him, the Cardinal's snowy hand clenched the cold marble railing of memory raw: months ago he had fallen two votes short of being the object of Papal adoration. Anonymous votes, perhaps not, perhaps gay-outing-fear votes, had sent him to the oblivion of policy drafting and financial audits for the Holy See—to this tiny office, this marble railing, this public humiliation. Lenza had been in the top three. *I was top three; then top two . . . so close doesn't count. Envy is a hungry beast—like an eviscerated African gnu—it lives for hours while hyenas and vultures have their fill. The gnu shakes helplessly bug-eyed while the steam from its innards curls skyward.*

Cardinal Lenza slowly held that same pale right hand toward the searing Rome sun. He admired smoothness, the smoothness of every finger, their paper-shuffle perfection. No scars. No sweat. A 72-year-old hand to be kissed, and often. The sun rose this day on his nothingness, but would set on his first calculated step to prominence—the Cardinal inhaled his own potency, an intoxication of vane glory mixed with a splash of fear as he savored the crunch of his afternoon Bruschetta and the self-assurance of glory to come.

Since the day the Papal conclave announced a name, *not his*—one who would be the new Pope Alexander, Cardinal Lenza had turned his face to a deadened servitude, no tics of joy or sorrow, only muted life, ashen and still. The days and weeks since had increased the conflagration of his deserved power robbed, his scrapping supplicants lost, and his treasure coffers denied. Consumed to retrieve his due, Cardinal Lenza devised a curative to fix the agony of his present, in a context that the new Pope Alexander, anxious to legacy-build, would surely and innocently endorse. What better flattery than the ten greatest Popes of all time?

Cardinal Lenza stepped into his office from the tiny balcony and sat stiffly at his "also-ran," ostentatious Holy See desk. "Isn't this interesting?" Father Timothy, his third personal assistant in so many weeks, a stubby man of stumbling word and dull mind, had the unsavory job of fluttering nearby and scraping the Cardinal's oft-silence for bits of direction. Word had spread quickly among the Papal staff about the difficulties of working with the "also-ran" Cardinal, but Lenza knew that the mental challenges and toadying of this priest *(what was his name again?)* would serve for now much better than the two sharper wits before him. "What do you see here?" Lenza extended his arm with the document while at the same time leaning away from the subordinate priest-smell.

"The ten greatest Popes listed in a *History News Network* article from 2005."

"Yes. It does a good job of succinctly laying out each Pope's priorities. Take a few minutes to review the text and then tell me which one you think would be the strongest voice against XTREM if he were alive today?" Cardinal Lenza enjoyed the fishing, the trap set—so easy. The left corner of his mouth strained to muster an encouraging upward curl, giving his acid-wash face the pretense of humanity. The priest might almost think his opinion mattered.

Father Timothy, from fear of landing himself back in Isernia (in his mind a Parish on the backside of Italian rock pile), cautiously spoke, "Maybe Blessed John XXIII (1958-1963). It says that John *was the most beloved, ecumenical and open-hearted pope in history. . . His encyclical on peace was addressed to all people of goodwill -- within and beyond the Catholic Church. This Pope renewed the faith and reached out to the world, radically changing relationships with other religions. Timothy could read, slowly, but he could.* Is that correct?"

"Perfect. That is what I was thinking." Lenza needed this oaf in his camp. *Step one . . .*

"Right now, call my cousin Geoffrey Lenza at this number and connect me."

"Yes, your eminence. Stateside number?" Father Timothy breathed relief. Timothy's newly-earned halo just scraped the jamb as he sidled cross-ways through the ornate door taller than two of him. He might last here. No need for number four. He wondered what time it was in Chicago.

"Yes, Chicago."

The Cardinal's cousin from Chicago had long decided to forgo the priestly route of Catholic service (much to his family's deep and public chagrin) and had instead routed himself into partnership at the Chicago Catholic Supply Company, which because of Geoff's chemistry and marketing expertise, now held the market product share for 78% of Catholic entities worldwide. The Cardinal thought his cousin both loathsome and enviable—much to admire and use both their advantages. Get him on the phone, get it done, and move on.

"Hello, Geoff, everything fine here. Been a long time. Sorry for the hurry-up, meeting with the Pope later today to present an initiative and want to bring you some business at the same time."

"What's in it for you?" Cousin Geoff knew the Cardinal well.

Cardinal Lenza's mouth tightened its edges while he mustered a calm but measured response, side-stepping his cousin's question. "I am going to propose that the Holy See proclaim a Catholic World Peace Day. Politically, we must avoid the dirt of the XTREM global fray, but our silence is also not advantageous."

The perfectly manicured nails of the Cardinal's left hand were pounding out Verdi's *Triumphal March* on his much-waxed, oaken desktop.

"To glorify the Catholic World Peace Day, a special green incense mixture would be used during the *Peace Be with You* portion of the Mass in every Catholic Church worldwide."

"Why green?"

"*Psalms 1:3--Such a one is like a tree planted near streams; it bears fruit in season, and its leaves never wither, and every project succeeds.* Immortality, my dear cousin."

Geoff's silence did not deter the Cardinal. "Chicago Catholic Supply Company will be chosen to manufacture the incense that will burn green in every Catholic mass held on the Day of Peace."

"You can get that done?"

"Yes, the *also-ran* has some leverage."

More Geoff silence. Verdi's *Triumphal March* got louder.

"Send me the cost specifications for incense manufacture, packaging, and delivery as soon as possible. Fair market costs—bury your finder's fee and my consulting costs somewhere, but be generous to both of us." *Step two . . .*

The Rome heat broke with an early-afternoon shower, each drop like a bit of dishrag scrubbing the pavers of supplicant smell and shoe scuffery. God knew how to clean up the dirty . . .

Cardinal Lenza met with the Pope late in the afternoon that day and presented his comprehensive plan for the new September 24th Catholic World Day of Peace during Sunday mass that would coincide with the annual September 21st World Day of Peace. "Your Holiness, this is an opportunity for you to be compared with one of the most famous Popes of all time. You cannot only walk in the footsteps of the Blessed John XXII, but you can also forge a new path against the tyranny of XTREM today."

Pope Alexander had had a long day of meetings, blessings, and pleadings. The new and embattled Pope was looking for opportunities to rise out of the naysayer ashes in these few months. Under different circumstances, the Pope most likely would have sought other council and studied the proposal longer. Instead, his fatigue and guilt over the *also-ran* in front of him cast the die in favor of Geoff and his cousin.

"As I recall," the Pope reflected, "John XXII renewed the faith and reached out to the world, improving relationships with other religions and their leaders. I am inspired not to be silent like Pius XII did during WWII. The Vatican did not speak out against the atrocities against the Jews in Germany. Now we have XTREM."

Alexander, like many before him, was not immune to the narcissistic creep of flattery and his image in history books yet to be written. "Did nothing" had lacked appeal and integrity, odd but honest bedfellows.

The Cardinal's perfectly unstained thumbs started twirling, and a short snort of glee escaped his stony lips, "If you sign off on approval today, tomorrow I can move forward with the plan."

"Well done, Lenza. The Vatican Communications Department will arrange the worldwide announcement as per protocol. I will make this announcement in person on television as well as radio. Grateful for your forethought. Take care of the rest of the details. Keep me posted. The days are long and expectations high."

On January 1st, Pope Alexander, with Cardinal Lenza standing behind his left shoulder, made his Papal proclamation. "As Christians and Catholics, we cannot watch thousands slaughtered or forced to leave their homes in the Middle East because of religious persecution without action appropriate to our mission. As a symbol of our unity in peace and support of World Peace Day on September 21, 1.2 billion Catholics will pray worldwide during a special Sunday mass on September 24 for end to all terrorism, especially the recent atrocities of the new terrorist splinter group XTREM. During mass, as congregates give each other the sign of peace, they will be embraced in green incense, signifying global harmony."

As Pope Alexander addressed his Catholic universe, Verdi's *Triumphal March* throbbed in Cardinal Lenza's mind over and over, the tempo pounding the pavers for what was to come . . . his immortality born from green incense. *Step three . . .*

Chapter 2 - University of California Berkley

A continent away, Cardinal Lenza's self-glory road was in for some unexpected aid or interference, depending upon one's reflection in the mirror. . .

Established in 1868, the University of California, Berkeley (UCB), ranked globally for biology and biochemistry publications, enrolled over 27,000 undergraduate and over 10,500 graduate students, several thousand international. The UCB campus was, therefore, a diverse-population-rich environment for real-world discussions and experiences. Within the labs of this prestigious institution and while the Cardinal plotted in Rome and Washington stewed over the XTREM Paris disaster, two Berkley graduate students had plans of their own that, unknown to them, would collide the present with the past.

Steven Habid's parents had emigrated from Syria to the US before he was born. His prolific professors deemed this lanky, 5'10," 25-year-old one of the brightest biochemistry students in their department, one who (with their endorsement) would go far in the field if he stayed the professional course they would design for their benefit and his.

One bio-chem lab joker (they were few) continued the public geek-bullying Steven had known since grade school. The classmate never spoke directly to Steven but his lab partners with just enough venom volume so that Steven could hear and pretend to ignore. "What say we stir up some new pop-bottle eyeglass cleaner for those 18th-century Sunni glasses? Kurd glasses? Sell online to the International Association of All-That-is-Muslim-Nerd and make millions!"

Unconsciously, Steven's right-hand index finger pushed his horned-rim specs back up the bridge of his narrow, dented nose. *He thought that which he could never bring himself to say, "Test-cheating sludge, stealer of others' work, brain-fart child of fools."* Steven could only look up and blank-stare his abuser, his same strategy since 5th grade—that and running like hell from the bus to his front door before the neighborhood kids could begin another "pummel-the-alien" kid episode. Blank stare and run . . . blank stare and run. At the Berkley labs, however, Steven had no place to run and didn't want to, but bullies past and present birthed his susceptibility, at any cost, to please people who showed him any positive attention.

Twenty-four-year old Darcy Oban clutched Steven by his mortal and immortal soul, and he had as yet no care to get free. It was not a physical clamp but a psychological one. It was irrelevant that he was Muslim, and she was Catholic. Darcy's father had also emigrated from Syria like Steven's, but his US-born wife was a devout Catholic who would not be faith-swayed. Darcy was also a promising biochemistry graduate student, a strategic commonality with Steven as he would later learn. Both graduate students benefitted from the financial privilege of parent wealth, leaving them to focus totally on graduate work, avoiding the struggle of the "work-to-to-pay-the-bills" unfortunates. Advantage, intelligence, and hatred—a potent mix that would eventually make its way to Stan Pace's door.

When Darcy first met Steven in their graduate cohort several years ago, it was over an isolated lunch in a small, oak-dusty café that would become their new harbor near the Berkley labs. The Tarter Café was a Muslim klatche for the privileged, a small societal cosmos, where students of "like" ethnic and/or socio-economic background, language, and behaviors created safety zones, much like immigrants to any new world. The fall-buzz campus had the new-student smell and bustle of hope. Steven's stumble-words focused on the dark, long-haired beauty across from him, one he could never *have*, but could twist himself into pretzels to please. Pleasing would be enough . . . more than he had ever known.

"What happened to you after 9/11?" Darcy knew the bond of shared wounds and how to use them for her plan ahead.

Steven did not look up from his Chicken Biryani and Moose Drool, mindlessly pushing the rice and bay leaf in a constant reel, a bit faster when his embattled geek voice choked the words. "Stayed inside—several days. I did not understand why or what we were watching on TV. My little boy world came to an end that day. When I went back to King Elementary. I had loved school, but nothing was the same after 5th grade. Camel jockey. Carpet pilot. My two best friends, Ray and Toro, hung in for a while, but they got scared off. I was called Muslim scum, bomber, and God-hating pig. I cried every day and night for a while. Then one day, no more tears, only hate. No argument, only hate through junior high, high school, and now here. My parents faded into wallpaper, dissolved like tablets in sludge water. I still miss Ray and Toro. I still miss my parents as I knew them before 9/11. Survive and hurt back? Why don't I leave this country? Where would I go? It's all I know, but I hate what I know."

What he could not tell Darcy were the memories that no drink or pill could dim. Steven wanted to remember his boyhood pals (he actually had them) more than the bullies, but his mind was stronger than his will . . .

"So you had your mommy tattle on us to the principal, shit head," said whispered one of his 6th-grade tyrants. "Careful, Stevie-boy. Payback coming, camel-fucker." Classmates in 8th grade ramped it up. "Have trouble in the airport getting through security? We'll just call you Checkpoint Cut Butt." Then came the near-drowning. School day tormentors stuck Steven's head in a toilet, flushing it as many times as the 4-minute passing period would allow while chanting "Dune-Coon-Go-Away-Soon." The cold water turned his glasses into head pinchers, his nose crushed in porcelain and red-stained swirly. While Steven actually saw more students who physically looked like himself by high school, it did not change the daily battle. Muslim hate-mongering escalated to a beating that would one day send Steven down the barbed hole of underground Syrian radicals. "You smell somethin'? Arab stink." Thugs from a nearby high school were on each side of Steven, pushing him back and forth like pinball, one hitting high, the next hitting low. Hard boot bruises, something breaking. Steven tried to fight back, but five against one . . . when the posse finally bored of its prey, sweaty fingers grabbed his wallet, car keys, and clothes with a few swift kicks to the groin and a go-back-where-you-belong goodbye.

Darcy only knew that today, the only extra-curricular activity outside of his bio-chem studies that captured Steven's time was attending Muslim student gatherings on the Berkley campus. He also read every print and online text about XTREM that he could gather without drawing undue attention from anyone who might be watching.

"His eyes have the anger I need—dead-black eyes behind coke-bottle rims. I don't have to touch him to get the plan in motion," thought Darcy as she leaned her long neck in motion with Steven's fork through the rice. "How about a sip of beer?" Darcy hated beer, but she knew that asking him would make him feel important. She was repulsed by Steven's weak, no work hands but their scraggy fingers that could mix the formula she needed. She knew Steven was the radicalized loner she needed to take back the hurt, and not just his hurt. Darcy kept her silence. It belonged to her and her alone. . .

California evening breezes and an approving moon surrounded the young scholars as they headed to the bio-chem lab later that evening. Smaller groups of students were a tangle of arms and legs moving to the nearest bar scene. "Bootylicious" by Destiny's Child and Lee Greenwood's "God Bless the USA" drifted from dorm and apartment windows in a strangled chorus collision strangely welcome in Darcy and Steven's silent steps.

Of the many students from all over the world who came to Berkley in hopes of Dr. Pace's selecting them to complete their graduate studies under this purview, Darcy and Steven had earned that privilege two years ago, and while the publically marble-like professor did not leak favoritism, he had taken a special liking to the odd-duck pair. They both seemed gifted but mundane, independent, yet needy. Dr. Pace not only admired the young scholars' scientific methodologies but also trusted their professional intentions.

Academic researchers around the globe considered Dr. Alden Pace, the 20-year head of the Berkley Biochemistry Department, a brilliant biochemistry scholar, credible and admired in a highly competitive field. His famed biochemistry program was more popular than ever, and Dr. Pace felt the continued pressures of publishing often, teaching effectively, and raising funds. His wife, Beulah, scoffed at his frets. Their life was secure and happy with many more blessings than sorrows. When her husband worried about Stan, Mrs. Pace would often use the same old line, "Stop worrying. God will see to it."

Darcy and Steven were now six months away from their Master's degrees and moving on to corporate jobs or Ph.D. degrees. As a result, Dr. Pace needed their final Master's project proposals. To that end, he had scheduled a meeting with them after hours in the Gilman Hall bio-chem lab, the hub of his professional life for the last two decades. As a result, Dr. Pace had grown long-accustomed to the familiar door squeaks and stuck-drawer scraping that accompanied the architecturally regal but tired infrastructure.

"As per the Dean's prior approval, you can complete a Master's project together that is of sufficient scope to justify credit for each of you. Project ideas?" Dr. Pace scanned both their faces as he prepared to take initial notes in the same brown leather binder he had used since day one at Berkley. The doctor wanted to hear his patients speak and speak well.

Darcy proceeded to pitch the proposal about which Steven was worse than vague, "In one of your classes last year, Dr. Pace, you mentioned that your son is the Director of the Center for Disease Control. Would the Center consider allowing this Department to undertake what some might consider a controversial project? In addition to our publications, the CDC might also be able to use the results."

"No surprise that you are looking for national and maybe even international recognition for your research. What is controversial?" Dr. Pace had a long history of allowing students to stretch research boundaries with the Institutional Review Board. He saw in Darcy's face a new persistence that he felt the need to support.

"Dr. Pace, we don't have everything worked out yet. Darcy may have jumped the gun a little." Steven's glare did not go unnoticed by either Darcy or Dr. Pace. While Steven wanted to please the girl, he could never have. When it came to his studies, his I-Will-Show-Everyone O' Meter had had the tendency to move up the charts, especially if he felt patronized. Steven went further to reduce the size of his bruised ego, "Could we submit our proposal to you within the next few days and then copy your son at the CDC? In this case, the project will most likely need both of your approvals in addition to IRB sign-off."

Dr. Pace's marble face melted a bit at the enthusiasm of his charges. Too many of his colleagues avoided the classroom. He found young learning the refreshment he needed for his thinking and work. "Get your proposal to me as soon as possible. I will determine whether, when, or if we submit it to the CDC. Fair enough? Long day—time to head home."

When Steven could no longer hear Dr. Pace's steps scuffing down the hallway on his way out, the grad student uncharacteristically verbalized his hurt, "You kidding? We aren't ready to discuss this. We haven't even agreed that this is what we want to do! You think I am just going to go along with this thing, just because, because I, I . . . ? I am tired of people speaking for me—making decisions about who I am and what I am supposed to be." Steven clutched the slate lab tabletop like a lifeboat, talking at its emotionless surface—much safer than Darcy's cold, judgmental eyes. Even though he smelled the familiar stink of Darcy-control, and its foulness repulsed him again, he could not escape it. He hated that which he did not want to escape.

"You are so talented. Steven, this project will set you on the professional path that you have always wanted, right? You will get published in the best journals and present at conferences—the envy of every Berkley wannabe." Darcy never apologized. Her puff-up strategy caved him—again.

Steven's hand clamps fell from the slick slate in empty clenched fists, false in triumph, true in frustration, "Tomorrow, we write up the project together. Don't present anything without me ever again." Wish words at best. Darcy had won again, but Steven was far from knowing the weight of the prize she really sought.

Steven was also ignorant of two important Darcy details. First, she had attended Mass two weeks previously and heard an announcement from which *her* idea for their biochemistry graduate project was born. Pope Alexander had proclaimed a special Catholic international day of peace to be celebrated during Mass on September 24. During the *Peace Be with You* ritual, priests and altar servers would use green incense developed especially for the occasion, a first in the history of the Catholic Church. Second, Darcy's continued attendance at Mass since her childhood disguised a deep loathing for all that was Catholic, like a child who continued to love and live with a parent who had struck her every day for decades. She went every week, waiting for the Virgin Mary to come to life and kick some priest butt, or maybe St. Something-or-Other would swim the Vatican moat on her behalf.

"Father, there were two--of them. On the beach below our house on the Raker's Bluff—you know, the one not far from here?" Eight years ago, sixteen-year-old Darcy was not polished at confession but confident that her Parish Priest, Father Aubry, would help her with what she had carefully hidden for weeks from her parents, especially her mother. Mrs. Oban never tolerated imperfection. Never. All things, all faces, all actions must be faultlessly creased in the World of Oban. No dimples in the varnish, no wrinkles in the linen. Darcy could not say, *"Father, forgive me for I have sinned."* If being half-Arab were a sin, maybe she was a walking sin after all. Darcy just needed the Father to listen, to help, to fix.

"Yes, I know that location. What two? What happened?

"The sun was almost gone, Father. Mother and dad were at another club dinner, and I needed a break—a walk on our beach. Lots of homework, you know?" Darcy's thin fingers nervously combed her long black hair over the front

of her gray sweatshirt, wishing to anywhere else, wishing it had never happened or happened to someone else. Who cares if it is someone else? "Our beach is private. No tourists, you know. They were waiting behind the big rocks, you know, further down the beach."

"Did you know these boys?"

"Yes, from Sacred Heart, same as me. They came new this semester—they might have been from a public school. Not sure."

"Had you talked to them before?"

"No. They talked to me, at me. Don't know why me. I am not the only Arab-looking student at Sacred Heart . . . they called me Al-Qaeda's slut, Muslim whore. They kept throwing 9/11 at me like it was my fault. They weren't the only ones, just the worst."

"Did you tell anyone?"

"I sort of told science teacher. Mrs. Bertrand just said, 'Ignore them, Darcy. Boys are like that sometimes. Just keep your head down and work hard.' She gave me a thumbs up on my way out the door."

"So what happened on the beach?

Darcy sat in the coffin-dark confessional. She closed her eyes, and the movie played again, as it had played over and over every day for the last 12 days, slow-motion, fast-forward, clear, then grainy. Darcy saw the boys from Sacred Heart come up from behind the rock pile up the beach ahead of her. The tall one walked crooked, like an old man; the other shorter one lumber-walked. Windbreakers flapping their high school frames, they started moving her way—

slopping slowly, but she could tell they moved with purpose, with infantile, deadly angers. She knew. They knew. Darcy's Burberry sandals spun and dug into the coarse Lake Michigan sand—please, house, hurry up and be there. Faster. Run. Move. Mother and dad, be there, please. Just once. Not me. Not now. They dragged Darcy off the beach to the base of the cliff, into the marram grass and Pitcher's thistle, out of sight and sound. "School on the beach, bitch." If she screamed, Darcy did not hear it. If her virgin body ripped pain, Darcy did not feel it, and if the boys fist-pumped following their two-hour Arab girl-assault-lesson, she did not see it. God sent only the lapping shoreline waves as gurgling witnesses in the Michigan twilight.

"They hurt me."

"Did you tell your parents or call the police?" Darcy's 16-year-old mind could not grasp or notice that Father Aubry had no interest in knowing exactly what the Sacred Heart boys had done to hurt her.

"No, they said they would tell everyone and mother and dad. They said they took pictures. I don't know." In the darkness of the confessional, Darcy could not see the dead-blankness in Father Aubry's face, nor could she know of Jimmie, Ralph, and Sergie, three of the many young boys who had suffered the priest's physical violations behind Parish doors. Darcy waited, waited to unclench her tight-fisted anguish with help from God's word.

"God sends us trials to test our faith. Pray for his grace, and go in peace, my child. I absolve thee from thy sins in the name of the Father and of the Son and of the Holy Spirit."

Darcy heard the confessional door quietly and quickly open and close. What she had come for had fled. In the months to come, her mother continued to provide Sacred Heart whatever financial supports Father Aubry requested, the "beach" boys moved on to yet another school at semester's end, and Darcy's fists stayed coldly clenched.

After eight years of silence, Darcy intended that the Catholic Church would soon pay its penance for that confessional day long ago, the day of Father Aubrey's flight . . . Steven Habid's part would not be printed in the penance program. There would be no applause and no encore.

Chapter 3 – Present Day / Atlanta, Georgia

The Centers for Disease Control and Prevention (CDC) is the leading national public health institute of the United States. The CDC is a federal agency under the Department of Health and Human Services and is headquartered in unincorporated DeKalb County, Georgia, a few miles northeast of the Atlanta city limits.

After the bombing of a Russian airliner, an attack on Paris, and then the San Bernardino massacre, and the promised threats from XTREM that Washington, D.C. was next, Dr. Stan Pace, Director for the CDC, called the department heads together, as directed by the President, for a review of policy and threats. Dr. Pace was unique in that after medical school, he enlisted in the Army as a doctor, graduated from Ranger School, did two tours in the Middle East, and then rapidly advanced to the CDC director's position. At 6'2" and 225 lbs., an athletic build, handsome, dark complexion, and single – he was a most eligible bachelor, as well as an intelligent and skilled leader. Everyone at the CDC respected him.

As the meeting began, Dr. Pace opened with, "Needless to say, what happened in Paris and California was unexpected, undetected, and a terrible tragedy and….."

Harold Cummings, a department head, interrupted, "Stan – while I know this was terrible, it wasn't a threat as described in the CDC's manual of responsibilities. We have enough to do without looking under stones that other agencies are already doing."

Stan understood where Harold was coming from, and he was concerned that they all might be using tunnel vision as they looked at the vast CDC scope of responsibilities, "Let's not be so narrow in our thinking, folks. French officials have one of the best agencies for detecting threats to their country globally, and with all their expertise, they missed this one. I want to review all our threat assessments under our authority and any other threats to be examined and reexamined. As you know, in our own CDC manual, which I'm sure you are aware of, but that I am reminding you – we have been very wary of a covert chemical attack on our soil as it is very easy. XTREM has the means and the money to make this sort of attack possible. Let's look at our own words in the CDC manual of our responsibilities."

Terrorist incidents in the United States and elsewhere involving bacterial pathogens (3), nerve gas (1), and a lethal plant toxin (i.e., ricin) (4) have demonstrated that the United States is vulnerable to biological and chemical threats as well as explosives. Moreover, recipes for preparing "homemade" agents are readily available (5), and reports of arsenals of military bioweapons (2) raise the possibility that terrorists might have access to hazardous agents, which have been engineered for mass dissemination as small-particle aerosols.

"Our plan contains recommendations to reduce U.S. vulnerability to biological and chemical terrorism --- preparedness planning, detection and surveillance, laboratory analysis, emergency response, and communication systems. I want to focus on working with the FBI closer than we have been regarding ears on the ground and not just reaction to an incident. Prevention is the keyword at this point," Stan barked with a tone that might have been a little too much! He wanted everyone in the room to try and feel what it would be like to be in Paris as a blindsided agency.

"Ok, Dr. Pace," Debra Matson, another department head, finally responded. "We need to set up secure daily video conferences with the Department of Homeland Security to hear what it is doing, whether activities are related to the CDC or not. I will take care of that." Fingers started to move, eyelids shutter-flicked, and tongues licked lips—there was bureaucratic life at the table after all.

Director Pace's neck craned slowly right and left to check body language for signals of support, silent disagreement, or downright sabotage. While he was not convinced that Harold gave a rat's ass about anything but his every-two-minutes of smartphone dopamine hits, Pace was grateful for what appeared to be a Cabinet table of mostly intelligent, forward-thinking, and dedicated leaders.

"Appreciate that, Debra. Tomorrow I will bring President Sutton up-to-speed at a special meeting of the NSC." While Stan's team knew that the President oversaw the National Security Council (NCS), they did not realize that their leader was President Carol Sutton's former lover and confidant, a role which Stan vigorously hid on the one hand and strategically used on the other.

The meeting adjourned with everyone having an area to explore, contacting people, and most importantly, checking on the chatter from 80 listening stations across the globe, which included 19 in Europe. As Pace stretched his long arms across the empty, sagging conference table, he slowly pressed his trigger finger over days' old wrinkles in the once-white dress shirt too long in the wearing. He closed his sleep-deprived eyes in thoughts he did not share with the team. *Why is there not more chatter out there? Digging in all the right channels? God, need a drink—Beefeaters on rocks. Surely no one on this team could be rolled, bought. Paris had no warnings. What if we don't? What dumb shits believe that silence is golden? How is Carol—need to see her.*

On his short, cramped, and oft-used flight to Washington and to avoid plane chit-chat, Pace buried his nose in old-but-goody readings like old friends who never talked back. On this February hopper flight to DC, he re-visited a passage from the crumpled paper copy of Bill Joy's 2000 article, Why the Future Doesn't Need Us: How 21st Century Technologies Threaten to Make Humans an Endangered Species:

"Bioterrorism is an attractive weapon because biological agents are relatively easy and inexpensive to obtain, can be easily disseminated, and can cause widespread fear and panic beyond the actual physical damage.[2] Military leaders, however, have learned that, as a military asset, bioterrorism has some important limitations; it is difficult to employ a bioweapon in a way that only the enemy is affected and not friendly forces. A biological weapon is useful to terrorists mainly to create mass panic and disruption to a state or a country. However, technologists such as Bill Joy have warned of the potential power which genetic engineering might place in the hands of future bio-terrorists."

This was precisely the kind of thinking that kept him up at night and made him shiver. Of course, the terrorists won't care who dies, which is different than an army fighting against another army. Stan had to stop reading this type of literature as it only scared him more, but Joy's view was accurate.

After three martinis and a ribeye at the Washington Hyatt Regency, Pace shower-drained his troubles as he pondered the next day's NSC meeting. As he leaned against the slick tiles for support and balance, the rhythm of steam-scalding water shot did its best to calm Stan's muscles and mind. Eyes shut saw flashes of Iraq and Afghanistan tours—more and more frequent as XTREM upped its carnage, leaving body parts in villages he had once helped secure. Eyes shut saw soccer balls and shoes for kids and built schools now evaporated by XTREM-delivered suicide bombs, land mines, and rocket fire. Eyes shut saw old friends lost, former patients dead, and apartments leveled. Up his nostrils, the shower steam delivered odorous oil and mortar musk. Shower-Sleep-Shower-Sleep. . .

I know this is textbook normal. Who doesn't come out the other end of war shit without some type of Post Traumatic Distress Syndrome (PTSD)? No bastard I know. Four simple letters—like ABCD—like shit that never flushes. Ranger training my ass. Hope Carol is OK. God, I need her. NCS tomorrow. If the shower would only stop . . .

Chapter 4 – Washington, D.C. – White House

The National Security Council meeting started at 10:00 a.m. in the White House West Wing Situation Room, a 5,525 square feet opened by John F. Kennedy in 1961 to provide on-time, sensitive security intelligence, and crisis support to NCS staff and the President. Over the years and through Presidents with differing needs, the space had been upgraded to be more technology-savvy: large screens for global communications, privacy booths for sensitive phone calls, and switch-on frosted glass to hide the inside view from the outside view. Pace likened the NCS meetings to his filling a plate with every entrée on the national security buffet table, a painful but necessary bloat to ensure as much as possible accurate cross-communications and strategic decision making. When people entered the Situation Room, they seemed to swell inches taller and swag feet wider.

Pace was predictably early, a lifetime habit of promptness no matter what his condition, intending to spend a few minutes with President Sutton; however, not this day. "So nice to see you, Director Pace," greeted her assistant with a judgmental I-know-why-you're-really-hear tone and demeanor. "The President will see you *after* the meeting." For a milli-second thought, he could smack the smirk off his face and nail it to the wall behind him like an anti-Playboy Bunny calendar. Bad idea—Carol had screened dozens to find this trusted bureaucratic sprout, and she liked him.

Iron-face Pace covered his disappointment as he moved aggressively to the Situation Room. There Stan was joined by the Vice President, Secretary of State, Secretary of Defense, Chairman of the Joint Chiefs of Staff, Director of National Intelligence, National Security Advisor, White House Chief of Staff, and White House Counsel. Everyone, as per protocol, stood when President Sutton entered the room.

Sutton typically dressed in the politically appropriate apparel of structured, muted designer suits, chicly conservative shoes, and minimalist jewelry. The 5'5", 52-year-old widowed mother of two, was admired on both sides of the aisle, not an easy task that she never took for granted. The President had lost her senator husband six years previously after a feisty but futile battle with stage 4 (metastatic) melanoma. They had been an envied power couple politically, and now Carol Sutton had to navigate Congress and the world stage as one, not two. Except now for Director Stan Pace—long-time friend, lover, and lifeline.

Stan and Carol had become lovers after last-minute gin and tonics together before her journey down the Presidential candidate road: pre-Secret Service, pre-White House pressures, and pre-daily microscopic publicity. As Sutton walked to the situation room, she remembered that night—her husband gone, her future unknown, and her accidentally running into Pace at Smithy's, a small warm pub that welcomed all souls, happy and troubled. She had embraced his chiseled kindness and absence of "so-sorry-for-you" face. Their private get-togethers in the White House living quarters were, with the help of mummer-than-mum White House staff, a rare best-kept secret that both President and Director had agreed to keep for now.

It was six years later he and Carol had become lovers that just happened after a spur-of-the-moment drink together. While she was older than Stan, it didn't make any difference. They had known each other for years. Since this was before her taking the Presidency, the secret service was absent from their first encounter. Now they were treating their get-togethers at the White House living quarters kind of like Monroe and Kennedy, with the exception that neither Stan nor Carol were married!

Although President Sutton wanted to grab Pace and slake him on the Situation Room conference table, she entered absent a glance in his direction and played her Presidential role with restrained perfection as always. "Be seated, everyone, and good morning. We have a lot to cover, but I specifically want to know, since our last meeting, if we have any further insights into the current means of communication that XTREM is using other than normal channels. They must be using something that the Paris specialists, as well as ours, cannot detect. Director Harvey, please begin."

Matt Harvey, the Director of National Intelligence, was always prepared, succinct, and honest, qualities that Sutton admired and trusted. "Madam President, of the four forms of communication that none of our current monitoring picks up, the most likely method used by the new splinter group XTREM is global e-sports, a form of competition using video games. Competitors text each other during sessions, but after they close the games, the messages are gone.

EXTREM followers can quickly receive and send attack plans—locations, targets, times, etc. that we cannot track because those systems never intended to have a trail.

E-sports can take many forms like multiplayer, individual games, team games, etc. The gaming systems like Nintendo-Switch, Microsoft Xbox, and Sony PlayStation 4 Pro are available worldwide and easy to use. While *PS4* uses the internet, tens of thousands of gamers play at any one time across the globe in small groups, and large arena competitions. Paris authorities have solid reasons to believe the recent attack there was planned via e-sports."

"So will Sony be able to help us in any way?" asked the Chief of Staff.

Matt replied in a very quiet and somber tone, "To decrypt communications using *PS4* is really difficult – even harder than *Whatsapp*, another forum. Clearly the terrorists are using *PS4,* knowing that it is almost impossible to decrypt even with Sony's help. We are working together to see if we can streamline the process. We have our best tech teams working on this 24/7. The company says there is a back door, but very hard to decrypt. The National Security Agency/Central Security Service (NSA/CSS) employs our best code makers and codebreakers and they are working around the clock on this situation."

Stan Pace's clenched, rock-solid jaw betrayed his bewilderment. "How can such a simple tool like a game be used to get around the world's best monitoring? Around the clock had better be enough. For our part, yesterday, the CDC started to increase monitoring of regular channel chatter regarding chemical attacks. But if the terrorists are on the dark web or on a game, our monitoring is useless." Stan felt his fists tighten as his tone got sharper and louder—then a quick body shudder. *Keep it down, Stan ol' buddy. Don't embarrass yourself in front of these political mucky-mucks, bottom feeders. Don't want Carol to see me like this. Dead meat around this table.*

Stan was amazed that such a simple tool like a game could be used to get around the world's best monitoring. "This seems to me to be a serious snag and one that we have to try and crack," he stated, "and just yesterday, the CDC started cranking up monitoring for chatter regarding chemical attacks as everyone knows that we are vulnerable in this area. But if the terrorists are on the dark web or a game, our monitoring could be useless." Stan was wondering if others were as worried as he was. A quick shudder went through his body which signaled his PTSD trying to creep into his thoughts – some screams – some cries for help…

"I agree, Director Pace," said the Secretary of Defense. "We are working across agencies and countries to come up with solutions to these monitoring issues and will gladly include the CDC's tech folks. If the best hackers in the world, who are now on our payroll, can't find a way into these systems, then no one can." The round-in-circles dialogue continued for an hour until it spent with little resolution.

On her way out, President Sutton said in an aside to Pace, "Stop by my office— ten minutes?" He briefly studied the slight worry lines that had graced

Carol's face the last time they were together. He was proud of her success yet wanted her to need him, just him, in every way.

"Stan, have a seat. Just 20 minutes." Knowing the public nature of this brief meeting in the Oval Office, President Sutton locked her eyes on Stan's with professionalism and grace. "Great to see you . . . thanks for attending the NSC meeting. You aren't a regular member, but for the near future, I have asked that you attend. Ever heard the saying *Truth to Power?*"

"Madame President . . ."

She quickly interrupted with an impatient wave of a well-manicured hand, "Carol, Stan. We know each other well enough, yes?"

"Madame President," Pace feet-shuffled in the stiff Oval Office chair, the one he had squirmed in many times, but the one he wanted to leap from and whisk Carol into the private residence quarters. Was their dialogue in this room recorded or videoed? By Carol? Surely not. By others sharpening knives behind her back? Maybe. Paranoia plague had no cure. "It just doesn't feel right in this office to call you Carol, and no, I haven't heard *Truth to Power*. New U-Tube thing? Congressional bathroom joke?"

Sutton lovingly rolled her eyes. "*Truth to Power* is a simple concept named by Quakers in the 50's. It simply means that my Cabinet or the NSC or you, for that matter, will tell me the truth and not what you think I want to hear, no matter how brutal. A leader needs to hear unfiltered information. Not sure I get the whole truth. Maybe my gender makes it harder for some of the alpha males, to be honest. They might be afraid they will be disciplined by a hormonal, hysterical Oval Office mother."

Stan choked on laugh one and then again on even bigger laugh two, "Madame President, you can say "truth to power" in Washington with a straight face? Christ o' mighty. Not enough shovels to scoop the piles of non-truth out of this town. Have you said to these folks what you just said to me?

"Not sure I want to let them think I don't trust them, but I sometimes wonder."

"Tell your Chief of Staff. You are close to him, and you do trust him, right? Ask him to drop a hint with some of his trusted NSC members. It won't be coming directly from you. The word will spread faster than the latest tax cut bill. But don't be disappointed if the congregation avoids your *Truth to Power* sermon. Little history in Washington of anyone getting more powerful by being truthful. Lying, yes. Honesty, no."

Unclasping her arms from a defensive position, President Sutton sighed in gratitude, "Ok, Stan. How is one of Washington's most eligible bachelors? Dating anyone?" Her eyes softened, pondering their relationship timeline, but personal curiosity momentarily cracked her Presidential demeanor.

Sutton enjoyed pushing Pace out of his safe space, and he knew it. Stan played along with a wink, "Casually dating two ladies with loads of moola. They both look like the backside of a bad day, but I remove all the lightbulbs, so it doesn't matter much. Might retire early and be a kept man with a capital K. Worth a try, eh?" Stan-Howie-Long couldn't remember his last date, but the tale sounded good and gave his Carol a Presidential chuckle.

"Take care of yourself as much as your agency. I know too well how hard that is. I need your opinions as we sort through the terrorist's communication systems. Help me make sure that the U.S. does not end up with the mess like France." Carol purposefully gave Stan that much-loved smile, the one that tickled his heart rate and weakened his resolve. They both knew and approved . . .

"Always a pleasure, Madam President, and I have your number," smiling as he left the Oval Office. *Only a convenience—that's it. I don't want permanence, let alone being White House First Man.* Stan was long-practiced at avoiding anything female that could stick to him. His justified independent loneliness might make a sorry epitaph one day or not . . .

Chapter 5 – UC Berkeley

Two weeks after their discussion in the lab with Dr. Pace, Steven and Darcy

met at his apartment on a Friday evening to watch a movie and talk. The movie

was used to mask anyone outside the door from hearing their conversations.

Their goal for the evening was to discuss their final master's project proposal,

which might be a front for a home-grown terrorist attack.

Steven started as he reported his "assignment for the evening, "I looked up an

article on ZIDBITS that identified the poison *polonium* as one of the deadliest

poisons on Earth. It doesn't take but a single gram to kill up to 1.5 million people.

So here Darcy, read this," and Steven handed her the short clip from ZIDBITS:

*Widely regarded as the most deadly, **polonium** has an LD-50 of 50 billionths per kg of body weight. This means that a single gram of polonium vaporized into the air could theoretically kill up to 1.5 million people. It's incredibly dangerous due to its intense alpha particle radioactivity. Alpha radioactivity isn't dangerous when it's outside of your body – a sheet of paper, or even your thick skin has no trouble stopping the deadly particles. It's when polonium enters your body that it causes havoc.*

"So my plan would be to purchase the polonium through UCB under the strict

controls that Professor Pace would require, which is expensive, and get it into the

fake smoke that they use when the LA Raiders NFL Team takes the field. I went

to a game, and the fake smoke goes everywhere as well as outside the stadium.

Since it only takes about as much that would fit on the tiniest pinhead to kill over

4,000 people, and it would take very little to kill everyone in the stadium. Can you

imagine what would happen to all the hospitals everywhere in LA if over 63,000 came in at the same time with the same symptoms – yikes. Everyone would be dead in three weeks, and there is no antidote."

He continued, "It is also a sort of famous poison as it was used to assassinate Aleksandr Litvinenko. So, what do you think, Darcy? We could use our master's project to order what we need, and the CDC would bless our study on how easy this could be."

"An interesting plan, Steven, and clearly would be a disaster of terrific proportions," she responded. "We would have to work out where we would purchase the polonium, how we would get the poison into the fake smoke mixture, and how far away we would need to be not to get poisoned ourselves. I think the death toll might exceed 100,000 by the time it escaped the stadium. Very interesting, Steven, but I have a plan to kill up to 79,000,000 Catholics thanks to Pope Alexander's proclamation of Catholic World Peace Day."

Darcy started after they had discussed Steven's plan a little further, "Steven, I have also thought a lot about something we could do that would be literally impossible to trace back to you or me." Darcy didn't tell Steven that if things went as she planned, she would leave to visit her grandparents in Aleppo, Syria leaving him to take the fall, and she wouldn't shed a tear for doing it.

"Please share it with me, Darcy. I do not want to throw away my hard work for my Master's degree for XTREM, and if your plan keeps me out of hot water, I like it already," Steven stated with a sorrowful tone looking down.

Thinking about what he just said alarmed Darcy as she was under the impression he was "all-in" as the Texas Holdem players say. "So do I hear that you are not interested in my grand plan that will shock the world?" she almost shouted over the movie. As an only child, she clearly demonstrated daily being controlling, cautious, structured, conscientious, and always an achiever and the "little adult" syndrome. She needed to push him a little to make sure he was a player and not an observer.

"Be calm, Darcy," asked Steven and replied, "Of course I am in – I am just more frightened now that things are escalating in France after the attacks and in Russia after the airliner was bombed. Now right here in San Bernardino, California. Every nation in the world is tightening its security and monitoring everything."

"You are very accurate, Steven, but they are not yet able to trace communications on the PS4 game player, which you have right over there under the TV," Darcy pointed. "I saw a report on the NBC Today Show Special Report regarding the *PS4* and the inability of the experts to decrypt the messages you send while playing a person anywhere in the world. It is my understanding that we can make contact with XTREM gamers."

"Interesting, Darcy," Steven said hesitantly, "I send messages while playing *PS4* games to my friends all the time. I never thought about it being used to thwart experts from seeing a message. So, we know we can hopefully communicate without detection if we know an XTREM member playing my games on the PS4, which I don't know how to find. So how does that help us with your plan, which you haven't shared yet."

Darcy said one word, "Ricin."

Steven gasped and said, "How?"

"We both know Castor Beans are rare but can be purchased, and ricin is easy to make," explained Darcy. "And my plan – our plan - will kill over 20,000,000 of the 79,000,000 Catholics in the USA all on the same day. The Pope has proclaimed that a special World Peace Day be celebrated on Sunday, September 24, 2017, at all regular Sunday-only masses. He even said that special green incense would be used since green is the universal sign of peace. The incense is the key. It will be used during the *Peace Be with You* portion of all the masses on that Sunday."

Steven gasped, "You are serious, aren't you, Darcy? Where did you come up with this idea?"

"I was reading about ricin, one of the most potent poisons around, making ricin, and a report came across CNN talking about a company in Chicago that has received the bid to make the incense sticks for all the USA Catholic churches. This company is just 28 miles from my home and sells all sorts of religious stuff to Catholic Churches, including incense."

Continuing, Darcy said, "With my background, I will send them how economically they can produce the green incense sticks using a solid stick as they use in Japan. It is pressed into a stick and can be broken into pieces. The bigger the piece, the longer it burns. The key will be using a ricin-infused green tint in the incense, so when hardened into a stick and lit will make the ricin airborne, which is its deadliest form. I will have to find a way to infuse this into their production process using Benzoin Gum Powder will give the incense a sweet and musky smell. We would need to use only an FDA-approved food color like Fast Green FCF, E143, which is a shade of turquoise. So, what do you think?"

"Wow – you sure have done your homework," Steven continued, "I'm somewhat familiar with the effects of ricin, and you have selected its most dangerous form – airborne. If I remember, ricin, when inhaled, has a terrible and swift effect on the body, causing your lungs to fill with fluids, develops a hard-bloody cough, and basically you suffocate and die."

"And Steven, the best part is there is no antidote," Darcy smiled, "I found this on the CDC's website regarding an antidote. The CDC's website states, 'There is no antidote for ricin toxicity.' So we can use Professor Pace's connection with his son to get permission to order a small number of castor beans and make a small amount of ricin to demonstrate how easy this would be for a terrorist to do on a larger scale. They, of course, wouldn't know that we would order enough to accomplish a much bigger task.

Steven pondered her idea and was thinking about how to get the castor beans when Darcy said, "So we just need to get permission and order the castor beans and have them delivered to the lab as part of our routine master's project at UCB."

"But Darcy, that exposes us and connects UCB to the incident when it happens, and as you know, they will look for castor bean orders and deliveries everywhere in the USA," Steven uttered alarmingly.

"You might have a point. We can have a small amount sent to the lab and the rest delivered to a warehouse that our friend has here in town. We don't need that much to make the ricin into a substance that can be infused into incense. When inhaled, an amount smaller than a grain of salt will cause symptoms within 4-6 hours after inhaling and death in about 24 to 48 hours. Can you imagine over 20,000,000 Catholics dying on Monday or Tuesday, September 25 & 26th, 2017? I got the 20,000,000 number from a Catholic report on the percentage of Catholics that regularly attend church. Hell – the number might be greater! It will make 9/11 look small and will clearly go down in history as the worst terrorist attack ever in the world. XTREM will take credit for the attack and threaten more unless their demands are met," Darcy was almost screaming with joy.

Steven quickly said, "Quiet, Darcy! We must be so cautious. Your plan is much better than mine was. We just can't tell another soul about this and never talk about it anywhere together except this apartment. We can use my kitchen to crush the beans and make the mush into ricin. As you know, it is undergraduate chemistry using filtering with water and some chemicals like hydrochloric acid. The recipe used to be on the internet, but in 2004 the Patent Office took it all off because it was so easy to make, but I have it here somewhere from one of my bio-chem class assignments."

"Will there be an odor with this process?" asked Darcy.

"We will burn some of our own incense during the process, and that will be the only odor, which will not even alarm any of my neighbors. They all smoke a lot of pot. No worries," Steven chuckled.

"Ok, Steven," Darcy said with excitement, "I will contact our warehouse friend and order the castor beans and split where they are to be delivered.

Darcy continued, "They usually come from Brazil, and our friend has contacts everywhere. For the money, he will do almost anything."

"Awesome," Steven responded. "So, I will contact my dad and tell him I need some money for my graduate project when I find out the cost of the beans and his silence. He never asks questions and just writes me a check."

They then sat together and wrote out a supposal for the master's project that they would submit to Professor Pace and have him seek approval from his son. Then it would all look like a very innocent project.

Darcy smiled, "Perfect!" She got up and left for her apartment, feeling great about the discussions. However, she remained concerned that Steven was weak and hoped that he genuinely was 'All-In.' She thought that if Steven did not stay committed to her plan, he would be after she had the ricin to take back to Chicago expendable. She dreaded that thought, but she was for sure, "all-in," and no one would stop her. She loved these feelings!

"See you at the university tomorrow, Steven," smiling, and she closed the apartment door behind her. Her thoughts were of triumph. Those that made her feel insecure and worthless would soon feel very differently. Many of these biased and "little" people just might be dead after 9/24. "Hmmm," she thought out loud. "September is a great month for terrorism and there is no antidote for ricin poisoning."

Chapter 6 – Freedom, Montana

Freedom, Montana is located about halfway between Great Falls and Havre on HWY 87, sixty miles either way. The city population is 800, with most of the folks living outside the small city limits. Average fall temperatures are 70-degree highs and 42-degree lows. About 80% of the residents are Catholic. Father John Warner is the Priest for St. John's Catholic Church in Freedom, Montana. He has been there for eight years and established himself as a beloved community member and a very understanding and caring priest.

Father John was of slight build, balding from the front to the back and a little overweight. He was excited to hear the Pope proclaim September 24, 2017, a World Day of Peace for all Catholics. The world was in quite a pickle. His adult religious study group had become sidetracked with everything that was going on in the Middle East with questions like, "Why would God allow such carnage and hatefulness." Of course, this brought up countless opinions with no real answers.

Father John was prepared for this discussion in his next session since he hadn't been previously. He took out an article from the *Catholics Called to Witness* publication written on February 12, 2015, by Elise Harris. The Article was courtesy *of the Catholic News Agency*. He shared a portion of the article;

An Iraqi priest currently living in Rome said that those living the nightmare of XTREM are tired of hearing talk about dialogue and human rights, and are ready to see concrete action on the part of political leaders.

'Like many other terms, dialogue is abused like the words democracy, peace, defending human rights and many other words, (They) are profaned because everybody talks about them, but in their hearts, they have other intentions, so who will do dialogue with whom?' Fr. Rebwar Basa CAN Feb. 2.

'I do not want to hear more from the people or responsible authorities about dialogue and peace. I want to see that people as happy and living a normal life. But what we can see now is that the whole of Iraq is in misery,' he said.

Each day that passes without changing the situation brings more destruction, suffering, and complication to the situation, the priest explained, noting that those suffering the most are the poor, including Christians, Yazidis, and other minorities who have no form of protection.

He told his parishioners in the study group that priests in the Middle East were starting to take a firmer stand against XTREM, which was one of the main reasons why the Pope had scheduled a World Peace Day for all Catholics. Father John was excited that this day had been established.

The next day, his excitement was put-on-hold when his brother, Jason, who lived in Ohio, called and said, "John – what are we going to do – we just set our wedding date for September 23, 2017, and you are marrying us. We have just paid the down payment for the reception which is nonrefundable. So now what? World Peace Day is September 24th, will you still be able to officiate at our wedding as planned?"

"Jason – I knew the wedding was in the planning stages, and now you have a date that is an issue for me," Father John paused and thought about his priorities. Clearly, marrying his brother was one of the most essential things in his life. He stated. "The only thing right now that I can think of is to ask the St. John's Parish council if we could move the Freedom celebration up a week to the 17th. I want to be part of the celebration so asking another priest to substitute is out of the question as we are so far away from other Catholic churches."

"Well... Freckles, you have to do something. If you don't marry us, it will break mom and dad's hearts as well as mine – com-on," Jason said, putting a guilt trip on his brother.

Father John was glad his brother couldn't see him as he was visibly bothered by the predicament and said, "I have a parish council meeting tomorrow night, and I will bring this up. I will call you after the meeting," John told his brother. "I'm sure they agree to the change."

Father John sat down and made some notes on how he was going to approach the council. He knew his brother was worried and calling him Freckles, his childhood nickname, meant he still loved him. He doubted the council would mind switching the date under these circumstances, but he had to be very non-assuming. To many in Freedom, the special Peace Mass was a nice gesture, but being so far removed from pretty much any violence or the politics of the country, let alone the world, made the Peace Mass just another mass.

The next night he explained everything to the council. They voted 12-0 to allow the celebration to be moved to September 17th at both Sunday morning Masses without much discussion. Father John thanked the council, and when he returned to the parish residence home, he called his brother with the good news. His brother was pleased to no end and laughed, saying, "I knew you could pull that off Freckles!"

Chapter 7 - UCB / Castor Beans / XTREM

Professor Pace had set a meeting up with Darcy and Steven to review their proposal for their master's project. He understood that they were trying to make their project something that was really useful and could make a difference. He had run the project by Stan, who approved the proposal with a few requirements as long as the controls were very tight.

"Ok, you two," the professor began, "I have talked to my son at the CDC, and since they are working diligently on trying to look at every aspect of potential biochemical attacks on our country, he welcomes any results your project might put forth that would make our country safer. The controls for your project have to be really tight. I will approve all purchase orders, receive all materials, and the final ricin can never leave our lab for any reason. Your work on this project will always be behind closed and locked doors. Within the lab, your materials will always be stored in double-locked and sealed small vaults. My son said he would come and be present for your final defense. The CDC will then take the tiny amount of ricin with them for disposal. The key to the approval for the project lies within how easy it is to get these materials into our country, make the ricin, and demonstrate in your defense how easy it would be to develop a bio-chemical attack then."

"Awesome, Professor, and we can't thank you enough," Darcy had actually jumped out of her seat and hugged the professor and then backed up quickly, kind of embarrassed.

Steven was also delighted and shared, "We will get started right away, and we will make you very proud of our work Professor." So they both went out of the building and got into Steven's crummy old car.

Steven accepted the responsibility of locating a reputable source for castor beans through their friend, and as per Darcy's orders, paid in cash from his father's money. Their friend managed a warehouse/storage facility all in one and never asked questions about anything that went on in the facility. Two orders were placed – one small one was sent to the lab's address and the other to the warehouse.

Steven was present for the delivery three weeks later and made sure everything was loaded into the storage unit. The unlabeled 40 pound bags were easy to move and carry. It reminded him of unloading lawn fertilizer for his father in the spring. The other single bag was delivered to the Professor with appropriate shipping and documentation.

Each bag, when processed, would yield about eight ounces of ricin. Darcy had said she needed 5 lbs. of ricin that could be processed with liquid green dye to treat about 22,000 incense sticks. There were plenty of castor beans to accomplish this task. He texted Darcy with the word "Hi," which meant to call him.

Darcy called Steven on her cell phone and using the predetermined terms for the status of the castor beans so as not to trigger any USA upgraded monitoring. She said, "Hi Steven. I can stop by the grocery store and pick up dinner. Do you have enough salad (beans) and fixings?"

"Thanks for the call; Darcy and I do have enough of everything for a great dinner," Steven said, "See you soon."

Since Steven always carried or rolled his very used gray carry-on luggage bag for all his UCB materials, it was normal to see him come and go daily with the bag. It also was nice that one 40lb. bag of castor beans would fit perfectly in the carry-on luggage. Before their first meeting to begin crushing the beans, he had brought five bags of beans to the apartment. He also purchased all the chemicals that they would need. So, when Darcy got there, they would have plenty to work on. While waiting for Darcy, Steven had questionable thoughts, thinking out loud, "Do I really want to go through with this?

On the one hand, it feels terrific and energizing. But, on the other hand, it feels like I am going against everything my parents have raised me to believe." The many years of bullying and biases quickly won out as a knock on the door jolted him back to reality.

Darcy arrived, they lit some incense and began crushing the beans. By using this process, there was no real risk of contamination, but just to be careful, they both wore masks. "This is easier than I thought," Darcy said. At this rate, we will be done in no time flat.   She asked, "Where are you going to discard the remnants from our processing?"

Steven explained that he had plastic heavy-duty tall white kitchen bags ready to use. The bags just looked like regular kitchen waste. He continued, "There are four giant dumpsters on the street by that construction project on my way to UCB. The foreman has told the neighbors that they are welcome to use the dumpsters for their personal use for as long as they are there. So, the site is not close to either of our apartments, and lots of folks are dumping stuff there."

"Sounds perfect," replied Darcy. "Do you think we need to contact an XTREM higher-up? Let them know about our project? Then they can take credit for the unheard-of terrorist attack?"

Thinking for a moment and rubbing his temples, Steven answered, "I hadn't really thought about that, Darcy, but probably it would be a good thing to do. Otherwise, they would not take credit. And we really want them to. But how do we want to make contact? I still don't know how to set up a *PS4* game with an XTREM leader, and I don't dare ask any of my friends even at the mosque how to go about that!"

"Neither do I," Darcy barked. "We can't take the chance and start asking questions. I have a cell phone number of a friend in Aleppo at the University that I know is a low-level member of XTREM. I can call her and ask her to relay a very short and encoded message to XTREM leadership. Something like '9/24/17

World Peace Day' will be exciting for the world. I'm sure there are millions of folks chattering about World Peace Day, so ours would not trip any red flags."

"Perfect," Steven said with a smile. "Our plan is really coming together! I may have sounded luke-warm originally, Darcy, but I am so excited now!"

There was a loud knock on the apartment door. Steven sat straight up, and Darcy froze. "Who's there?" Steven said with a shaky voice.

"It's your favorite next-door neighbor Gary. Open the damn door – I know you are smoking weed; otherwise, you wouldn't be burning incense."

Steven choked back his fear and looked at Darcy and whispered to her, "What do I say now?"

"Tell him you have a lady friend with you and can't be bothered right now. Then, he'll figure it out and leave," Darcy hoped.

Steven repeated what Darcy said, and Gary laughed, "That never stopped you from letting me in before you, dog! Come on. I just want a puff, and I'll leave."

Darcy whispered to Steven, "If that asshole gets in here, he will ask a million questions and blow this whole thing. We can't clean it up fast enough for him to come in. So get rid of Steven, or we may just have to kill him, and I wouldn't hesitate. I'm not kidding."

Steven felt faint, "Gary – I'll bring you a joint in a minute."

Gary relinquished, "Fine – she must be a prude, Steven," and they could hear him close his apartment door. Steven went to his dresser, grabbed a joint, walked it across the hall, knocked on the door, and gave it to Gary, who was most appreciative.

When he returned, Darcy whispered, "That was close, and tell me more about your weed stash and girls in the apartment? I thought you didn't have time for girlfriends?"

"Well – about six months ago, I started dating a girl, and it didn't go anywhere. She brought some joints with her and left them here so her roommate wouldn't find them. That's all, Darcy," Steven responded, almost like a boy with his hand caught in the cookie jar.

"Any other surprises you want to share, Steven?" she smiled.

They worked late into the evening mashing beans and using chemicals to make the mush into ricin. When they were done, they cleaned up, disposing their gloves, masks, and remnants from their work into the garbage bags. Darcy reminded Steven that she was going back to Glencoe, Illinois, the next week for spring break and was going to check into the Chicago National Catholic Supplier, INC. There had to be a way into the company – somehow!!

Steven said that while she was gone, he would continue the processing of the beans.

The next day Darcy made the call on Steven's cell phone, claiming hers was low on battery power. It was not, but it was part of her plan to make sure nothing could be tied to her. The call was less than two minutes to her friend in Aleppo, Syria. She felt good about the call, just talking about the big World Peace Event in America, and she knew that XTREM leadership would understand that something big was going to happen in the USA on that date, not just celebrating peace. Like San Bernardino, Darcy and Steven were not on anyone's watch list and were just average, intelligent, caring college students.

Darcy thought after the call that the United States insured religious freedom as part of their foundation, and now that freedom will kill tens of millions. How poetic was that! She almost frightened herself with her uncaring attitude towards really everyone.

In Clarksville, Virginia, on 215 Burlington Drive at a former candy factory, one of many Department of Homeland Security (DHS) listening stations picked up Darcy's call and classified it as nothing significant. Cyber Security Analyst Charles Nulty keyed the note that went into the database, "Another World Peace conversation – Berkeley, California to Aleppo, Syria. Initiated by cell phone number 312-555-1682 / owner Steven Habid. Time of call 22:16 EST - 90 seconds – nothing unusual."

Chapter 8 – Glencoe, Illinois / Chicago National Catholic Supplier, INC.

Darcy arrived home in Glencoe via taxi from Chicago, O'Hara Airport, on Saturday. Glencoe is 24 miles North of the Chicago loop and is an upper-middle-class community right on Lake Michigan. Darcy's home was on a bluff overlooking Lake Michigan, and she always looked forward to sitting on the back porch looking at the solid blue water for as far as a person could see. The sound of the waves and the constant breeze would always clean her mind, even after the assault on the beach in high school.

She would walk over to the rock wall overlooking the beach where a scene from *Ferris Bueller's Day* off was filmed. While she was only a one-year-old when the film was released, everyone in Glencoe considered that movie a classic for years to come.

In high school, she was a model student with stellar grades. Sitting on the back porch, listening to the waves, doing her homework was always a treat. The memories from the homecoming dance and rape attack still were burned into her thoughts and overshadowed some of her fondest memories.

Her parents were always excited to see her, and she shared everything about her master's work progress at UCB. They spent the rest of the day Saturday and Sunday catching up on family and her father's business ventures. While her parents were talking, Darcy's mind drifted. She was thinking about what was to come and that she may never see her parents again after September 24th, and the attack was successful. She never told Steven that as soon as she was finished infusing the ricin somehow into the incense mix at the Chicago factory, she would fly to Aleppo, Syria, to visit her grandparents. From there, she was uncertain where she would end up, but she was positive that US authorities would backtrack the sequence of events, and probably her name would come up. Steven's name would then come up through her cell phone use and the questioning of her parents in due time. Steven was weaker than she was and would tell them all he knew about Darcy to save himself.

Monday Morning, Darcy borrowed her mother's car and drove to Evanston, where she picked up the train and went down to the Northside of the loop where the Chicago National Catholic Supplier was located. She wanted to see the building, walk around it, and might even go inside as there was a retail store in the front.

The retail store was a perfect way not to be noticed as two other people had entered. So, Darcy went in and browsed. There were tons of Catholic items everywhere. Crosses, bibles, rosary beads, incense, pictures, trinkets – just about anything a person could ever need that wanted to display their faith or read about it.

A sales gal came up to her and asked, "Can I help you with anything?"

Darcy turned and said, "No – I'm just looking," she stopped speaking for a second and said, "Nancy Martens – is that you?"

"Oh my gosh...Darcy Oban. Can you believe that two Glencoe high school friends meet like this? It has to have been what – six or seven years since we have seen each other. What brings you here?"

"Well," Darcy was scrambling for a saleable story, "My mom is always looking for interesting rosaries, and I didn't have much to do on spring break, so I drove down here to look around. More importantly, how have you been.?"

Nancy looked back at the other worker and said she was stepping out for a moment and to please watch the store, "Let's go outside so we can talk. It is so nice."

They went out and sat on a bench by a bus stop. Nancy shared, "Wow – this is so cool. So – after high school, I went to the University of Wisconsin as a business major and going to summer school and taking sixteen hours each semester graduated in four years, which is hard there. Then I came back to Chicago and lived with a guy thinking we were made for each other, which didn't work out. So now I work at this company and only help in the retail side about one day in the week, and I do marketing the rest of the time. How about you, Darcy?"

Darcy was careful as she shared, "Well – I am in graduate school as a bio-chem major at the University of California at Berkley and hope to finish soon. No boyfriends, just have been plugging away in school for the past seven years. It sounds kind of boring, but I just immersed myself in the university and have loved it."

Nancy stopped her from continuing saying, "Darcy – I have to get back in there. Here is my card with my cell phone on it. Can we get together before your break is over and catch up?"

Darcy smiled as this was music to her ears and said, "I'll call you tonight. Thanks, and what a coincidence, Nancy." They both gave each other a formal hug, and Nancy went back into the store.

On the way back to Glencoe, Darcy worked on ideas that might allow her to get the production schedule for the incense sticks as well as how she might then get into the production area. It wouldn't take more than five minutes to pour the liquid ricin into a vat. But getting that all accomplished would require a very close friendship with Nancy. That would start this evening on the phone.

She was still thinking about how glorious it would be for people to die from ricin inhalation. Since ricin was a toxic protein, it attacked cells and stopped the body from producing protein, causing the body to start shutting down, especially the gastrointestinal organs and lungs. She imagined watching a person viciously coughing up blood and losing the ability to breathe, which would cause certain death. However, if the person did survive, their organ damage would cause them a lifetime of pain and suffering. She thought, "Welcome to my world of suffering."

"So was she a terrorist?" she looked up the term "terrorist" on her cell phone when she got home and read the following, "Section 802 of the USA PATRIOT Act (Pub. L. No. 107-52) expanded the definition of terrorism to cover "domestic, " as opposed to international, terrorism. A person engages in domestic terrorism if they do an act "dangerous to human life" that is a violation of the criminal laws

of a state or the United States if the act appears to be intended to: (i) intimidate

or coerce a civilian population; (ii) influence the policy of a government by

intimidation or coercion; or (iii) to affect the conduct of a government by mass

destruction, assassination or kidnapping. Additionally, the acts must occur

primarily within the territorial jurisdiction of the United States, and if they do not,

may be regarded as international terrorism."

"Well," she thought, looking out her bedroom window, "I meet every aspect of

the definition of a terrorist. I will go down in history for eternity." Thinking some

more, she estimated that the US Population was about 323,000,000. When

22,000,000 Catholics, or more, die after September 24th, that represented at

least 7% of the entire US population. She smiled and reminded herself that there

is no antidote for ricin poisoning – NONE.

Chapter 9 – CDC Headquarters – Atlanta

"Stan, can I talk to you a minute?" asked Jack McLaughlin, the communications expert at CDC, as he poked his head in my office.

"Sure, Jack, what's up?" Stan asked.

"That's the problem, Stan. Besides the Russian airliner, the French attacks, the Turks blowing a Russian fighter jet out of the sky, San Bernardino, and all the chatter surrounding these events, our homeland is too quiet," Jack stated in a frustrated voice. "Usually, there is a lot more data we are trying to decrypt in conjunction with all our other agencies working together, but in the last three weeks, there has been really nothing worthy of even a hint of any terrorist activities. The 175 identified radicals in the country that are being watched and monitored are pretty much silent and doing nothing to attract our attention in any way. Just is really different."

"Jack, President Sutton has issued many warnings for the police and all Americans to be on alert, and the 'See Something Say Something' campaign is taking hold in almost every state. She isn't doing this because there isn't any intel. She is doing this to crank up millions of eyes in the USA." Jack was not the kind of person to exaggerate anything or to set off alarms without cause, so his angst did bother Stan.

"I know all that, Stan," Jack continued, "but in my morning teleconference with all the directors of communications in every agency, they are saying that they do not hear much either other than a few idiots trying to become famous by making some threats. They are monitoring tweets, Facebook, and every other social media. They are even monitoring people for unique physical attributes and other biometric information. Hell, I understand that they can scan the way you walk as an identifier and archive it if you are on a watch list. With everything going on here and across the pond, don't you think we should hear more here?"

"I realize that you are concerned, Jack, and I agree that it seems odd," Stan said with some conviction, "do you want me to weigh in at the White House and see what I can find out?" Stan knew that he could contact President Sutton and chat about what Jack was bringing up.

"Look, Stan," Jack barked, "I know you are close with the President, and I am not asking you to jump over any line-in-staff protocol – I just don't want any agency to be caught off guard like what happened in Paris or California. I think about what bin Laden wrote in notes to his followers that we captured in his home, and that was 'attack soft targets, easy targets, unsuspecting targets, and take your time'. We thought we were doing a great job until 9/11 happened, and no one had thought of using airliners as weapons until it happened. Now, look at what we put into place at all our airports with TSA security. We had to react instead of being proactive. What is out there that we are now missing? That's my concern."

Stan shuttered as Jack was making his points, and while the CDC's responsibilities were well defined, every agency was supposed to expand their focuses and try to think of the unthinkable. What could we not be thinking about? Is it right in front of our eyes, and we are blind? God, he hoped not!

"Ok, Jack, I will bring up your concerns tomorrow with the President and see what her reaction is. Clearly, she is briefed in much more detail than we are daily. I think you are asking if there has been a 'What if' discussion in the DHS and what is on that list that we haven't seen."

"Thanks, Stan," Jack thanked me and left my office. Stan punched in the President's Personal Assistant's phone number and asked if the President had any time for tomorrow's video conference. The answer was a maybe, and she would call him back. She then asked if he could tell her what the topic was about, and Stan said, "status of national security." Jack's concerns radiated in his mind to the point that he started making mental lists of potential ideas that hadn't been considered.

His paper was blank, and then one thing danced across his thoughts. The CDC manual states that the biggest threat the country is open to and probably could not stop will come from radicals working in states that have vast spaces, sparse populations, and homegrown extremists. All the agencies focused on dense population areas and significant public events and not much on sparse areas. While the Boston Marathon, San Bernardino, and Paris were dense in population, large geographical areas in the US could harbor extremists planning attacks to be carried out in remote areas. The most manageable threats to carry out would be chemical, biological, or IEDs.

Stan called Jack in his office and shared his thoughts. He agreed and said again that we needed to start looking through the lenses that the radicals and extremists were looking through, not ours. He continued saying that we were trying to do this but still may be too narrow a field of view. Stan told him that he hoped to talk with the President tomorrow.

That night as he tried to fall asleep, the voice in his mind kept repeating what Jack said about bin Laden – 'attack soft targets, easy targets, unsuspecting targets, and take your time' – his last question to himself was, "What are the softest, easiest, most unsuspecting targets in our country?" Finally, he fell asleep, thinking he would get a think tank together, draw up a list, and compare it to what he was sure already existed.

Early the following day, the President's Assistant called Stan and said that while the President would like to talk with him, she was swamped, and could the conversation wait? "Of course," he responded. "I can talk with some folks at the DHS. Please tell her not to be concerned, and thanks."

Next, he contacted his friend at the DHS and discussed his concerns. He indicated that they too were exploring everything possible and that the CDC's folks were well briefed on anything and everything concerning terrorism issues. Stan thanked him and went back to work. The "what ifs" are being considered by everyone. He just hoped that our lenses were wide enough to see what we currently could not see. It was such a different world than when we planned our responses as well as detection manuals. Stan was worried that we weren't keeping up with the terrorists who schemed 24/7 and only needed to be right once. We needed to be right every minute of every day.

Chapter 10 – Chicago National Catholic Supplier, INC.

On Monday morning, May 15, 2017, Darcy Oban was back in Glencoe, getting ready to visit Nancy at the Chicago National Catholic Supplier, INC. (CNCS) at 10:00 a.m. to tour the facility. Nancy was excited to show her newfound, old acquaintance around. Their previous short phone conversation resulted in this very welcoming chance to scope out the place and establish a very close relationship with Nancy, her ticket into the facility in the future. Before departing from Berkley, she and Steven had finished working the castor beans into ricin and disposed of all the evidence of their work from his apartment. She paid for her rent through the summer, so no one would think she wasn't returning, especially Steven.

The ricin was packed safely in one of her suitcases that she loaded into a rental car on her drive back to Glencoe, Illinois. In a checked bag at an airport, Ricin would no doubt be detected, so she had rented a car. The drive to Glencoe from UCB was beautiful, except for Nebraska and Iowa, which were flat and very dull.

Darcy showed up promptly at 9:45 a.m., introduced herself to the receptionist in the lobby, who said Nancy was expecting her. A few minutes later, Nancy came into the lobby, "Hi Darcy – great to see you, and I'm excited to show you the digs of our organization. Actually, it is kind of boring, but the production area is pretty cool. Half of the stuff we buy wholesale, which is my responsibility."

Darcy responded, "This will be fun, and I'm taking you to lunch afterward without any objections!" Nancy nodded and smiled.

"Here is my office and the rest of the folks responsible for running the company. I doubt you have heard that we were low-bidder for the Pope's special green incense display this September's Catholic World Peace Day. That was a big deal, and I was part of the bidding process, which made me feel great!"

"So, how big a deal is that?" asked Darcy.

"Well – after all our expenses, we should realize about $400,000 as we are the sole provider for all the United States Catholic Churches. That doesn't happen too often," Nancy smiled.

The offices were traditional, and everyone was hard at work as they passed this area. As they entered the production areas, Darcy tried not to look too interested but focused on the large vat that would have to be used to mix the final formula before it was poured into the incense stick forms for setting. She was glad she never was part of the original incense formula, which she was going to offer, as she was hopeful, they had it all figured out without her help, which obviously they had — one less thing to tie anything to her. The ricin in liquid form would be harmless and only lethal when the sticks were lit. She noticed that there was an outside exit door about 30 feet to the West of the vat.

"This is quite a setup, Nancy," Darcy chimed. "I'll bet the team on your project won't have to spend too much time getting it all ready with all this equipment. You probably have tons of security in here as well."

"Actually, Darcy," Nancy remarked, "Not too much need as really nothing of real importance is ever in here. We are an on-time delivery company, so we get what we need the day we need it and send out stuff the day others need them. We have never had a break-in or even any vandalism. The Northside of Chicago is really a pretty safe place. Sure makes me feel safe working here."

"Oh – also, we intend to put the incense job to bed the week after the 4th of July. Then, of course, we have to send them all out in little packages of two or three, depending on the sizes of the congregations listed on their order forms," Nancy continued as they walked around, "and distribution will be my responsibility. That will be tedious work."

As they walked, Darcy thought about CNCS's future after they were responsible for selling incense sticks, killing over 20,000,000 Catholics. No doubt they would probably go bankrupt, and probably some of them would be arrested as accomplices in all the deaths. She would be watching from afar how all that would play out as CNN would cover every inch of the aftermath for months and years to come.

"Fascinating, Nancy," Darcy smiled. "This is a bigger operation than I imagined. Let's go to lunch; I'm famished."

Nancy suggested a great corner diner and very Chicago style. They walked the three blocks getting there before the rush, and the waitress said to take their time-no hurrying necessary! Darcy started, "You know Nancy, it isn't every day that a company gets this big of a contract affecting every Catholic Church in the

USA. Have you thought about doing a story for the Sun Times? I always read the special interest stories that they run. You could give them a start to finish description. They really love Chicago stories."

"You know, I hadn't thought of that, Darcy, great idea! Nancy took out her notepad and jotted down some notes.

Darcy interrupted and shared, "In my world, we have to chunk everything down into small steps as we report on our experiments – like step by step, including the exact timeline for each step. I'll bet that might help you tell the story. It sure does for scientists." She hoped that Nancy would find this an excellent idea, but Darcy's reasoning indeed focused on something completely different.

"You are so right – it would be like storyboarding from the day the Pope proclaimed World Peace Day to the actual celebration!" Nancy couldn't write fast enough. Then she excused herself to use the restroom, leaving her master key on the table for Darcy to watch. Darcy quickly pulled out her phone and took a close-up picture of the key, and put her phone back into her purse.

Professor Pace had warned her regarding leaving or losing keys to the bio-chem lab. He always jokingly said from the quote he read, "A key that can be photographed can be copied." She hoped he was right, as that is precisely what she was going to do.

Nancy returned, and they headed back to CNCS. On the way, Nancy stopped and asked Darcy, "If I write up a draft of an article with some sort of timeline as a proposal for the Sub Times to consider, would you look it over for me please, please, please….?"

Darcy stopped her string of pleases, saying, "No problem Nancy. I'll get you my email, and you can send it to me whenever." Darcy was hoping that Nancy's timeline was exact, which hopefully would include the date the mixture would be mixing for usually 24 to 48 hours. After that, they would surely do a minimal run and light the incense up to make sure everything would work as planned. She was hoping that bunch would no doubt be saved to fill late orders after the main orders were all delivered. Then, if anyone checked, that initial run would be clean.

Nancy thanked Darcy, and the two each went on their way. Darcy was excited and now had to research how to get a key made from a picture. The internet was always a great resource, and when she got home, she would do some surfing.

The surfing ended up being so straightforward. She found a Popular Science article about an app for the iPhone called "Keyit." So simple, anyone could do it. She followed the easy instructions, and for under $50, she would have a functional key from her picture in one week. Crazy world we live in, she thought.

Nancy was a little off on the timeline that she sent, but not too far! The Sun Times had sent a business reporter over to interview Nancy and was impressed with the story and timeline idea and was willing to do a series of articles following the production and had also contacted the Holy Name Cathedral to finish the story during the Peace Be With You portion of the mass the special incense would be used. July was set as the testing of the initial 300 incense sticks. Darcy thought this was kind of fitting since the 4th of July being Independence Day. It was just kind of ironic in her mind! So, testing of the harmless sticks was set for the week following the July 4th break.

Darcy was in a sit-and-wait mode spending many hours sitting on the deck just watching and listening to Lake Michigan like she had done her entire life. She would miss these moments. Her mother joined her frequently, and they talked about the upcoming semester and what she might want to do after graduation. Darcy listened and responded like everything was normal and on track, which pleased her mother.

Darcy also called Steven to tell him that everything was on schedule and just go about his life usually, and she would see him in August at UCB. She kept the call short as she did not want to discuss their plan intensely with Steven.

Before the week of initial testing was to take place, Darcy needed to make sure that her new key for CNCS would work on that exit door not too far from the vat.

Finally, the date Nancy had listed on her timeline arrived to test the initial run of incense sticks. The entire team involved in the project sat around the conference table, each with a small portion of a three-inch green incense stick. They lit the sticks, and a very green smoke quickly emerged from each stick with the ordinarily sweet and hard-to-ever-forget smell of incense. Cheers and applause happened almost like a conductor given them a que.

The production manager, Charles, stood and said to everyone, "I am so proud of this team. From our response to the request for bids with all the specifications to our studying how we would produce the product to now actually testing the product – it has been quite a ride. Now we just have to mix the masterbatch after the 4th of July holiday, and Nancy and her folks will package everything and get them all sent out. This has been an important project and a special thanks to Nancy for contacting the newspaper for a special interest story featuring our company." Then, he said the team would get back to work in his typical scope and sequenced manner.

Nancy added, "I would like to take all the credit for the idea with the Sun Times, but my friend from high school, Darcy, actually brought it up."

Charles responded quickly, "Well, the next time you see Darcy, have her stop by so I can tell her thanks. Ok – let's get back to whatever." The meeting was over.

Nancy went back to her office, feeling very optimistic about the entire project. Finally, she was getting noticed for her work, which hadn't happened too much in the past. Next, she called Darcy to tell her again, thanks for the advice on the detailed timeline that Darcy had reviewed and that the Sun Times was on the story.

"Let's not wait so long again to get together," Nancy was still so excited.

"I'm all-in, Nancy," Darcy shared. "Do you have plans the week after the 4th? I see that the final stages of production will start on that Wednesday. You probably don't have too much to do at that stage. How about lunch that day?"

"Sounds perfect," Nancy said goodbye and hung up.

Now the trick will be getting into the facility Thursday night. Since there are no alarms, cameras, or guards – just stopping by and quickly entering through the door by the vat should be a walk in the park. That should only take five minutes tops. She would drive her parent's car down to the building Wednesday when she had lunch with Nancy and find a way to test her key in the lock since her vehicle would be in the lot adjacent to the door. She didn't need to open the door, just turn the key, so she knew it worked. The plan was coming together nicely.

Now Darcy had to check her passport to make sure it was in order and then asked her father if he would mind if she flew to Aleppo to visit her grandparents before the Fall semester at UCB began. He was excited, said yes, and even offered to pay for the expensive round-trip flight, which she knew he would do. Everything was in order now. She wondered if it was customary to feel absolutely no remorse for what she was about to do. She also didn't care one way or another.

The Wednesday following the 4th of July, Darcy met Nancy for lunch at the same diner they went to before. Darcy had parked in the lot next to the door leading into the production area. Their conversations at lunch centered on the fun Nancy was having with the Sun Times reporter, the pictures he was taking, the interviews with folks on the team etc. Darcy just let her talk and commented where appropriate. After an hour, they walked back to the building and said their goodbyes promising to get together before Darcy going back to UCB.

Darcy walked next to the building as she went towards her car. Instead of turning to go to her car, she stepped to the right and approached the door, which was only five feet from the sidewalk. She had filed the key to get any spurs eliminated, which it said in the directions to do when she received the key. Coming right up to the door, she quickly pushed the key into the lock, which went smoothly and turned the key, which turned easily and promptly removed the key and stepped back on the sidewalk, and went to her car.

She got into the car and didn't realize how stiff and tight her shoulders were from tension. Stretching, rolling her neck, and taking a few deep breaths, she started the car and drove to Glencoe.

The next night she asked her parents if she could borrow their car and drive downtown to just walk around and see the sites - something she had done a lot previously. They, of course, offered no objections. She was worried that at night in Chicago, anything could happen – even in neighborhoods that were deemed safe. So, she took her five-inch switchblade with her that she bought off a questionable guy on one of her breaks in undergraduate school. She never took it to UCB as going through the airports with it would cause her significant issues.

With everything in hand, including the packaged ricin in a bag, she drove off. When she arrived at the supply company, she drove to the parking spot in front of the door she needed to enter. Not wanting to draw attention from anyone by parking out of the lot and in front of the door, she walked to the door with her bag. The key worked perfectly, and while the area was dimly lit, she could see exactly where she was going.

She took out her mask and put on her gloves, opened the bag of ricin, and gently infused the ricin into the dye mix. The ricin quickly disappeared into the mix and did not change its color or consistency. She smiled as now; the only way the ricin would be lethal was when it was lit. Gathering the empty bag, her gloves, and mask, she went out the door, walking to her car. As she threw the bag into her backseat, knowing that she had to dispose of it where no one would suspect anything, she closed the back door and turned to open the driver's side door.

"Hey there – do you have any money for the homeless?" a very grungy, thin man was standing two feet from her.

Darcy was startled, jumped away, shouted, "Get the hell away from me right now, you idiot!"

"That's no way to talk to someone that just wants money for food. You obviously have a job at this business, and so I know you have money, sweetie," he smiled, getting a little closer to her.

This was a very serious problem. Now a person could identify someone coming into the business after hours even though a homeless person would be telling the story. When the authorities finally got to CNCS, they would canvas the area after finding that no one employed at the business had anything to do with putting the ricin into the final batch. This idiot was a problem.

"Ok old man, let's step over there, and I will give you some money," Darcy motioned to the right where there was a small tree in the parking separation island. As they walked there, she opened her purse and pulled out the switchblade opening it as she did, and stabbed the man twice in the stomach and under his rib cage to the heart. He went down immediately, groaning and grabbing his stomach, struggling to breathe. It reminded her of what she would like to have done to her rapists on the beach.

Darcy quickly, but not running, went back to her car and left. Now she had to not only dispose of her bag but wash her hands and get rid of the knife. Killing this bum was just a bump in the road to her. They will think it was just another Chicago murder in a parking lot not associated with CNCS. For sure, it would make the news as it was in a neighborhood that not too many murders occur.

She took the outer drive North looking for construction bins. About 2 miles south of Winnetka, a gas station was open, and there was a bin in the next lot for a construction project. So she went inside to the restroom, washed her hands, checked for any blood on her clothes, went out into the station and purchased a soda and a box of garbage bags, went to her car, placed everything in one of the green bags, and dumped it into the large bin and drove off feeling absolutely no remorse.

Two days later, she kissed her parents and thanked them for sending her to Aleppo and said she would see them soon. She knew that would never happen. Knowing that she had to tie up two loose ends after she arrived in Aleppo, she jotted down in her notebook two items to tell her parents the week before UBC's Fall semester started. They were expecting her to fly home that week: 1 – She was staying with her grandparents and finishing her Master's Degree at the University of Aleppo. And 2 – Notify UCB that she was not attending the Fall semester and to cancel her apartment. She left her personal cell phone in her bedroom desk, as she knew she would not need it again, and took her suitcases out to the cab.

"We are so proud of your accomplishments," her mom said as she hugged her before she got into the cab. "We will miss you, but your grandparents are thrilled to see you in person rather than on Skype!"

Her father also gave her a giant hug and said, "Darcy – you have come a long way, and I am excited about your future. Be safe, and we will see you in a few weeks." He gave her a peck on the cheek, and she got into the cab.

The driver took County Line Road to the Tri-State Tollway and turned onto Interstate 180 to Chicago O'Hara Airport. She went through international customs, waiting in long lines, found her terminal, and, when announced, boarded her flight to Aleppo, Syria. The fifteen-and-a-half-hour flight was not something she had looked forward to, but she had brought a book and would sleep some of the time. Her parents had sprung for a first-class round-trip ticket, so there was plenty of food, drinks, and attention from the flight attendants.

Her thoughts were of triumph and joy. Not ever seeing her family, friends, or America again was not on her mind. While unknown to her, Syria, XTREM, and everything associated with this new world was dancing across her mind as she looked out the window for the last time at the North American Continent. She hoped that some of the people who bullied her and treated her as a second-class citizen were Catholic. Screw all of them and closed her eyes, and slept.

Chapter 11 - UCB Start of Fall Semester

Steven had just learned that Darcy would not return to UCB for the Fall semester, and according to the registrar, she just had dropped out. He was panicked. What had happened – what had changed? His first thoughts were to see Professor Pace and explain that he was ready to present their/his master's project so he could graduate and move on. He called the professor's secretary and made an appointment for that afternoon.

He arrived an hour early to review what he was going to share with Professor Pace. He needed to be cautious. As he sat in the outer office, he calmed himself, took deep breaths, and waited. Professor Pace came out of his office and said,

"Welcome back, Steven. Great to see you. How was your summer?" as they walked into his office.

"Actually, pretty boring, Professor Pace. I did the finishing touches on our master's project, read a lot, and the summer just inched by."

He then stuttered a little and said, "Darcy has dropped out, and I don't know much more than that. I need to continue on our schedule to present the project this month as planned."

"Well – this is quite a surprise," the professor saw that Steven was very nervous. "Do you feel that you can present the project without her, or do you need more time?" He was stunned that Darcy had dropped as she was one of his stellar students with a very bright future.

Steven answered quickly, "Yes sir, I can, and I will. Everything is ready, and our lab has remained secure as required. We or I am more than able to present our findings, which are quite honestly a little alarming. Your son will be interested in how easy castor beans can be brought into our country and how easy it is to make ricin. It is quite a study, sir."

"Calm down, Steven. We can make it all work. I will notify my son of your situation and schedule a date for your presentation as I know he is interested in being present as previously planned."

Steven's back and shoulders relaxed; he sat back in his chair and thanked Professor Pace. Professor Pace shook his hand and gave him a fatherly hug, and told him not to worry. "Things like this just happen, and everything would work out."

Steven smiled and left the office much happier than he was when he arrived. He was, however, worried about the timing of his presentation and the soon-approaching date for the attack. As planned, he was sure that there was no way that he could be implicated. He kept telling himself this throughout the planning stages.

Professor Pace emailed his son and explained the situation, and asked him to send him potential dates that would work for him to be present for the master's project presentation. He sat back in his desk chair and wondered just what had

happened to Darcy to make her drop out. This just didn't make sense.

Chapter 12 – Freedom, Montana – September 17, 2017

Sunday morning, September 17, 2017, was ten degrees above average temperatures for Montana that time of year. Father John Warner surveyed the Ponderosa Pine long in needles and the Trilobe Sumac red-orange-yellow in emerging fall through his small but well-positioned pastoral office window. He had shuffled and reshuffled zealous paperwork to arrange the celebration of peace details for a 7:30 a.m. and a 10:00 a.m. Mass. He expected St John's would see at least 150 parishioners at St. John's Catholic Church that day, double the usual crowd. The extra donation byproducts would please his Eminence.

Sister Deb Miller, assigned to St. John's for many years, had called Father John earlier that morning with news that set him in a flurry. "Father John, can't make it today. You know . . . terrible head, just terrible." He knew well the too-often sounds of slurring and raspiness that woke up with Sister Deb after a heavy night with Beefeater London. Today of all days.

"Ok, I don't have time to deal with this now, but we can't afford to let this problem get so out of control that the Cardinal finds out. Bad for our business, you know. Just another thing to cover up. Just can't have it. Major day today. I will take care of it."

"You were counting on me. So sorry," Sister Deb wheezed as Father John hung up on her.

The bedraggled, newbie priest meticulously reviewed the order of the masses for the day, a long habit of over-organization: Introductory Rites, Liturgy of the Word, Liturgy of the Eucharist, and the Concluding Rights. His Homily was focused on important Peace Christ's time and today. This would flow nicely into the Sign of Peace following the Lord's Prayer.

Father John innocently prepared the incense sticks with his large paw-hands, one for each mass. *They don't look any different. I want to try a stick first to see what the green looks like but I only got two. Don't want to mess this up.* Normally the Church did not use incense during the Sign of Peace, but the Pope had proclaimed that incense burning a green color would be used in this section of all Masses held on the Worldwide Catholic Peace Day. Father John, by circumstance, had received Diocesan permission to complete his Peace Day earlier than every other parish—much to his misfortune.

Father John gently pulled open the doors of a dilapidated altar cabinet, much abused by at least four priests before him in the last six years. Inside sat a thurible, an ornate brass device suspended by chains into which he would put the incense. Father John would light the incense sticks inside the thurible and complete broad, single swings with the mechanism during Mass, first at the alter and then among the parishioners standing. *Will they notice the "green?" We put it in all the bulletins. They should. Need to press the wrinkles from my robe.*

At 7:28 a.m., Father John and two altar boys walked to the back of the church, and the Entrance began with organ triumphant *Help Lord the Souls-Belmont*. Father John said the Greeting and moved on with the Mass. He was proud of his

Homily about peace in the world, present, and past, and later, after the Lord's Prayer, he readied and blessed the thurible, crossed himself, and said a silent prayer. *Bless this day of hope. Bless Sister Deb in her time of need. Bless this Parish that it can thrive in my time. God forgive my selfishness.*

Father John lit the incense stick, made sure it burned adequately, and made single thurible swings around the altar. Before he moved into the 62-member congregation, he explained, "When Christ first broke bread with his followers after his resurrection, he said to them, 'peace be with you.' Today we ask for peace in our country as well as around the World." As Father John moved into the aisles of the congregation, he blessed everyone with more swings of the thurible. Their eyes follow the bright green incense. Cameras clicked. Children stood near the end of the rows, catching the green with tiny fingers. Father John felt the rapture.

The second mass was a repeat but more grandiose. Father John counted 91 worshipers with many a large pocketbook. Word had spread from mass number one—he noticed that the congregation contained many CEOs (Christmas, Easter Only) Catholics. *Green was good.*

The parish council president was delighted, and on his way out of the second mass stopped Father mid-baby kiss, "Tremendous service, Father. Being the "first" Parish to fulfill the Pope's wishes is such an honor. The green incense— great idea. I am also excited for you to officiate at your brother's wedding. I know how important it is to you. When are you taking off?"

"Bless you for the kind words. Flight is leaving Wednesday morning from Great Falls. See you when I get back, and thanks for understanding." When the sanctuary finally emptied and the last parishioner blessed, Father John took one more glance at his Blessed Mother Mary, thanked her for the day, and turned out the sanctuary lights, without knowing, for the last time.

Chapter 13 – Freedom, Montana – September 17, 2017 – Sickness

At 2:30 p.m. that afternoon, Sister Deb was feeling better. She had sobered up and stopped by the rectory to see how the peace celebration went that morning. Sister Deb was one of the kindest and most caring people anyone had ever met despite her secret problem. She knocked and entered at the same time into the kitchen and saw Father John sitting at the table, "So how did it go this morning, Father?"

He looked up, and she noticed he was pretty pale and said, "Really well, I think. We had over 140 folks attend, and pretty much all of them came down for donuts and coffee after the Masses."

"Father," she asked, "you don't look like you feel too well – kind of pale if you ask me."

"Oh, I'm sure it is a touch of the flu or something," he answered in a calm voice. "I'll be fine – just took some Tums and an Advil. I have to be ok to fly to my brother's on Wednesday."

"I do want to apologize for missing Masses this morning Father," she shrugged, "I know you know why I missed, and it is embarrassing, and before you say anything again, yes, I will get some help for my problem." She was ashamed of her behavior with alcohol issues. So many times, she went for months without a drop – and then she would fall off the wagon for no apparent reason. Sister Deb had read all the literature about alcoholism and knew it was a disease. That didn't help either.

"Sister Deb," muttered the priest, "Getting help in this town means that everyone would know you have a drinking problem. You will probably have to go to Shelby, which is only twenty miles away. They have AA meetings in one of the senior centers twice a week." Father John kind of grabbed his stomach and said, "I am really feeling worse. Now I am also having some shortness of breath – even a tight chest."

"Ok," Sister Deb said, putting on her pretend nursing hat, "we are going to the Freedom Health Clinic Emergency Room right now. I'm driving – let's go."

Father John did not argue with her. He knew he would lose that battle and probably couldn't drive the short distance anyway the way he felt. He climbed into the car, and they left for the center. When they got to the ER, Dr. Cindy Robinson, senior center physician and one of only three doctors in Freedom, looked up and said, "Well, Father John...what brings you into my ER?"

"My chest is tight, I can't get my breath, my stomach is upset, and on the way over here, I started coughing," Father gulped as he answered her.

"Let's get you into a bay and check things out," Dr. Robinson motioned to her left.

The doctor listened to the priest's chest, took his blood pressure which was 165/90 – a little high – took his temperature, which was 100 – looked in his ears, eyes, and nose, finding very little wrong in these areas, and said, "Let's draw some blood, get an IV going, some oxygen, a nitroglycerin pill, get a chest x-ray and do an electrocardiogram, Father John. That will give us a better picture. I don't like your symptoms. You might be having some heart problems. Is there a history of heart disease in your family?"

"Not that I know of," the priest responded in a weaker voice than Sister Deb had heard before.

"Lay down, Father, and rest while I have the nurse do the tests we discussed. Do you have any allergies to medication?"

Father John shook his head. "Sister Deb, you are welcome to stay if you like," Dr. Robinson explained. Cindy was very concerned with the numerous symptoms and told the nurse to start an IV and to get some help so one nurse could remain with Father John in the bay. He was only in his late 40's, and if there were family history, he probably would know about it.

The Freedom Health Center Emergency Room was rated by the American College of Surgeons (ACS) as a Level V facility. According to the ACS standards, this means that the Freedom Emergency Center ER would provide:

- Basic emergency department facilities to implement ATLS protocols

- Available trauma nurse(s) and physicians available upon patient arrival.

- After-hours activation protocols if the facility is not open 24-hours a day.

- May provide surgery and critical-care services if available.

- Has developed transfer agreements for patients requiring more comprehensive care at a Level I through III Trauma Center.

Five full-time nurses, two on duty at any one time, and one receptionist were employed by the center, which was attached to a twenty-bed unit. Freedom usually never had more than five patients in the overnight unit at any one time. Dr. Robinson had come to Freedom three years ago from Seattle, Washington, right out of her residency in Internal Medicine. She was single, 5'7", slender, in terrific shape with long brunette hair. She was well-liked by everyone in Freedom. Her family still lived in Seattle, where she grew up. Freedom was her first stop on her experience journey.

At 3:15 p.m., Cindy was walking back to see Father John with some of the testing results when a family of four came into the ER, all having similar symptoms as Father John. Cindy asked the receptionist to call in the other three nurses and one of the doctors in town. She was alarmed after checking each of the family members to find that they, too, all had the exact symptoms.

She asked the father of the family, "What have you all eaten in the past twelve hours?"

He responded, "Well, last night, we all had hamburgers, baked beans, and French fries. This morning we had toast and cereal, donuts after church, and some soup for lunch."

Cindy was puzzled. Unless the meat was spoiled, the other foods were unlikely to cause these symptoms. She asked, "Was the ground beef fresh, or had it been sitting out for a while?"

His wife answered, "I bought it yesterday morning at the grocery store with a use date or freeze date in five days. So, it was fresh."

Cindy asked the nurse to stay with them as she went to see Father John and Sister Deb, "Well, your electrocardiogram is normal, and there is no indication from the blood test that there are any signs of a heart attack. So, that is a good thing. Let's keep the IV going and monitor you, Father John." Sister Deb stayed right at his side in the bay.

No more than 10 minutes later, a young couple in their twenties came into the ER with the same symptoms. The other three nurses had arrived as well as another doctor. Cindy was now more than alarmed as she had never seen anything like this before. Dr. Hogan, who has just arrived, was briefed by Cindy. He, too, hadn't seen so many people all coming into an ER with the same symptoms and said to Cindy that they all must have eaten or been exposed to the same thing. He, too, was very concerned.

By 5:00 p.m., 46 children and adults were in the ER, and with only four bays, Cindy had opened the ten two-bed hospital rooms for the overflow. None of the symptoms was life-threatening. Cindy had called the Center's director to notify him of the situation. He was out of town at another facility that shared him as a hospital administrator and told Cindy to use her judgment but to call for help if necessary.

Cindy called in the third doctor in town to come quickly and assist the team. When he arrived, she brought him up to speed on the situation. He explained that he had been in the service and served in Iraq. As a young doctor in the military, he was exposed to all sorts of patient illnesses. He suggested getting urine samples and getting them to Great Falls as he knew that the hospital was part of the CDC's Laboratory Response Network (LRN). They were equipped to use rapid detection tests to determine what was going on since all the patients displayed similar symptoms.

Cindy called the Freedom Police Chief and asked if there was any way he could arrange the life flight helicopter from the Great Falls Hospital to come and take some samples to their lab for testing as she had an emergency in the making. He said he was sure they would accommodate Freedom. Next, Cindy called the Great Falls Chief Administrator, explained Freedom's dire situation, and asked for lab assistance, which he eagerly agreed to. He explained that to his knowledge, the rapid detection tests took six to eight hours to process. Cindy understood and thanked him.

By 9:00 p.m., 90 patients were sitting in all corners of the facility – in chairs, beds, cots, and on the floor on blankets. More were coming in. Cindy and her team were beginning to worry. While most patients were not in life-threatening conditions, some were getting worse. Wrist bands with numbers were assigned to all patients and entered into a database indicating a medical condition, age, sex, and location in the Center.

Sister Deb was standing outside Father John's bay when she saw Tommy and his family enter the ER. She rushed over to them and hugged Tommy, and asked his dad what they were there for. He explained that they had all started feeling ill with the same symptoms as shortness of breath and stomach pain. Tommy was holding his stomach and said, "It really hurts, Sister Deb." She motioned to one of the doctors passing by them and asked him to please take special care of the family as Tommy was one of her favorites.

The doctor, along with another nurse, put wrist bands on them and took them to the area where the overflow was being held. Sister Deb went with them quite concerned and tried to comfort them as much as she could.

At 12:30 a.m. Monday, Dr. Robinson received the words she both dreaded but needed. "Presence of ricin was initially confirmed. Toxin activity tests will take 48 hours." She stayed in the small conference room to make a call to a person she had met at the conference last year—Dr. Stan Pace, head of the CDC. Dr. Robinson quickly scrolled her cell phone for his contact information and gasped "thank God" when his cell phone number popped up. One of the topics at the gathering had been biological warfare, and she trusted his knowledge and judgment going forward. *3:45 a.m. his time—no matter—can't wait.* He would not want it to wait. However, Dr. Pace's contact information did not include the bedroom of the President of the United States.

"Yes," Stan did not recognize the number, but this was the "urgent call" line that only went to military, police, and medical staff. Carol had awakened to hear Stan's groggy voice. They had had a rare evening together, and as she brushed back her thick hair, she could hear his familiar voice, a man-voice she adored, wake up, and take alarm.

"Dr. Pace, sorry about the hour. Dr. Cindy Robinson from Freedom, Montana. We met last year in D.C. at a medical conference . . . presence of ricin in 50+ patients here in the last 12 hours." She could not control the fatigue and fear in her stutter-stumble words.

"Deaths?"

"Not yet."

"Organ shutdown?"

"No, nausea, sweats, chest tightening . . . excuse me, just a minute, Dr. Pace." He could hear a door rap and paper shuffling.

"What is it?" Leaning on a pile of starch-white pillows, President Sutton knew well the constant and necessary interruptions of their secreted lover-life.

Stan gently pushed her mussed hair from her worried brow. "Ricin."

Sister Deb, in the meantime, had decided to walk around the small Freedom clinic to help where she could. Halfway through the now 100+ patients, the Sister looked into the eyes of a familiar boy. Across the aisle, she saw a well-known elderly face. *Oh, my God. . . Oh, my God. . .*

Sister Deb first leaned on the conference room door and then knuckle-wrapped the "Staff Only" door. "Dr. Robinson, they're all Catholic."

"I heard." My team and I will be there in seven hours. Standard protocols. I will notify the Montana Governor, put additional emergency measures in place, and send immediate medical assistance from area hospitals that haven't already received."

Carol, "Need a helicopter to Atlanta to join my team for flight to Freedom, Montana."

"Carol looks like a ricin attack in Freedom, Montana. Over 100 people in overcrowded, understaffed small regional ER. No dead, but Great Falls Hospital Lab confirmed ricin. Governor Larry Hirsch will declare Freedom a disaster area so that he can mobilize National Guard. We will keep you and Security Council posted by the minute through our communications specialist. Press will be all over this like drunks at an open bar."

"God, Stan," the President gasped, falling back on her bed pillows. "Worst fears true. Ricin. Good Lord. Will do all I can from here." Carol's eyes said, *I want to come with you*, but her body stayed abed.

Stan leaned into her with a velvet-fist touch only he could give. Carol wondered how many that fist had injured or killed in the line of duty, or out of it. No matter. Despite their improbable situation, this soldier-turned-administrator would be her best and always.

"Careful," Carol ran her fingers over Stan's much-earned, deep-furrowed brow, and he was gone in the darkness. He smells of man, a hint of Creed Green Irish Tweed and sweat. No down-hugging could replace Stan or her late husband. These were narwhale nights, diving deep with no air.

As the President heard the helicopter rotors approaching the White House lawn, she quickly contacted Matt Harvey, Director of National Intelligence, with the details she knew. "Matt, Code 14."

"Acknowledged." Director Harvey would set national alarms in motion with all players needed. It had begun.

Stan darted solos across the manicured green of night and into a Boeing Chinook for the two-hour flight to Atlanta. He noticed media outlet vans and trucks just gathering at the front gate. Hungry for the latest disaster fodder, they would, with the sunrise, give the President's Press Secretary a merciless breakfast of questions and assumptions about the Chinook in the yard.

Chapter 14 – 30,000 Feet Atlanta to Freedom

Given the size of the only private airport in Freedom, Montana, the CDC team ordered a Gulfstream G650, 14 passenger jet for the 5 ½ hour flight. Governor Hirsch had mobilized that Army National Guard out of Fort William Henry Harrison, Southwest of Freedom – about 2 ½ hours away. The estimated time of arrival in Freedom by the Guard was mid-day. The Guard Commander and the Freedom Police Chief were working together. By early morning, all residents were notified to stay home – schools and businesses were closed, and the town was clearly in a panic mode. The unknown was their worst enemy. The press was also starting to arrive in Freedom, adding to the heightened concerns of the citizens in the community.

"Hi, it's Dr. Pace. I think we will land by 9:30 a.m. Dr. Robinson," he announced, calling her cell phone.

"Not a minute too soon, Dr. Pace," Cindy sounded tired, having been up all night. "Patients are Googling ricin poisoning and finding that there is no cure. And that death can occur within 36 to 72 hours of exposure, depending on how they were exposed. We still don't know how they were exposed. Sister Deb has indicated, as you heard, that everyone here is Catholic, and to make matters worse, Father John, the Catholic Priest, says that nothing out of place happened at church that he was aware of."

"Cindy," Stan tried to calm her down, knowing it probably wouldn't help, "Tell the patients that since we don't know how they were exposed, death is not always certain and that help is on the way. They are right, though; there is no cure for ricin poisoning. But, hopefully, it wasn't airborne and was digested. So they most likely won't die from it being ingested. Pretty hard to get it airborne."

"See you soon, Dr. Pace," Cindy almost started crying but realized she had to stay focused. Other nurses and doctors had arrived, as Dr. Pace promised. That helped, but not really. Watching her patients, many of whom were acquaintances, was unbearable.

"Dr. Robinson," Stan directed, "Two directions: 1) Order the physicians to immediately implement the DHS Response to a Ricin Incident protocol in the Guidelines, Section 3.0 until we discover how the patients were infected. Full polyethylene suits, gloves, surgical masks, and eye/face protection." 2) You must sleep—office, conference room, somewhere. We'll wake you when we land."

"This will really scare them for sure," Cindy said in a questioning manner.

"I know, but I think you have to make this call. As a Level V Center, do you have the suits?" He had to ask.

"Yes, we do, and we will gear up," Cindy responded. "See you soon."

Dr. Pace kicked around all the possibilities with his crew on the flight. Sunday morning Catholic Mass was the common denominator. Based on the information available, these 150+ people had common opportunities for ricin ingestion: during Mass communion wafers, communion wine, and after Mass coffee, water, and or doughnuts. What was the commonality for airborne inhalation? None of his crew members were Catholic, and Stan could not focus. His PSTD was retching in his brain again, triggered by Dr. Robinson's voice, choking his ability to make inferences, valid or otherwise. He dialed Freedom's Chief of Police.

"Chief, Dr. Stan Pace with the CDC. We need you to rope off the Catholic Church—sanctuary, rectory, the whole thing. Be as low-key as possible. No one is to enter the church, drink any water on the property, or touch anything outside without latex gloves, which need to be bagged. National Guard will join you within the hour."

Sister Deb watched Father John's labor breath inside what seemed to be a brand new but useless oxygen tent. *He doesn't look real—like a wax-man. Yet, the hands that lifted to help so many are still. Does he know I am here? Thank you, Father, for sticking with this old nun. What prayers do you need?* The sister could not stop the heart monitor next to his bed, turn its channel to a steady, deadline tone.

Stan's phone rang again – it was Dr. Robinson, "Hello, Dr. Robinson."

Dr. Robinson had not obeyed Dr. Pace's second order, and he knew she wouldn't.

"Dr. Pace, patient #1, Father John just died. Resuscitation failure. We have 152 patients and have asked the school superintendent to use the adjacent elementary school gym to house ER overflow. Attempt to keep Father John's death secret failed. Some patients who can still walk want to leave."

"Dr. Robinson, they can't leave under any circumstances—sedate them. So I will have the National Guard cordon off your center and the elementary school. No one leaves for any reason, and the Guard will stop them if they try."

Cindy paused and then said, "I know you are right, Dr. Pace, and I'm glad to have the Guard support as a few of the patients may not just take staying here lightly. God – what a nightmare. See you soon." Cindy hung up and just sat for a moment before she went back and consoled and helped the families in the clinic.

Sister Deb came up to Dr. Robinson and asked if she could use the clinic's phone to call Father John's brother Jason, a call she was not looking forward to.

"Of course, Sister Deb," she put her arm on Sister Deb's shoulder and took her to her office and set her behind the desk, turned and as she left the office, closed the door.

Sister Deb was old-fashioned and always had a small address book in one of her long skirt pockets. She pulled it out and, through her tears, called Jason.

"Hello, is this Jason Warner? she asked.

"Yes," was his response. "Who am I talking to?"

"My name is Sister Deb, and I am the nun assigned to your brother's parish here in Freedom, Montana. As you may know, we have had an incident in our town. After Masses Sunday, your brother felt ill in the afternoon, and I took him to the local clinic. Unfortunately, more ill people came to the clinic with the same symptoms as your brother a little later. I hate to be telling you this on the phone, but your brother died just a little while ago."

Sister Deb paused as there was no voice on the other end. Then Jason said, "Oh my God! This can't be happening. He can't have died. Oh, my God," and fell silent again.

"Jason – something terrible has happened here in Freedom," Sister Deb explained. "We don't know what or how, but everyone in the clinic that is ill is Catholic."

Jason stuttered a little and said, "You mean they all are sick, and they all are Catholic? Oh, my God!"

"I am so sorry for your loss Jason," Sister Deb knew Jason was devastated. "I will call you when I have some more answers. Unfortunately, I have to go and help others in the clinic." Jason crying, said he understood, would call his parents immediately, and they both hung up.

Sister Deb was glad that she was alone. She put her head down on her arms and sobbed. Then she got back up and went straight to where Tommy and his family were located. She sat with them, holding Tommy's hand. Her prayers for Tommy and his family were running through her head at light speed. So young, she thought. The cries from what seemed to be coming from everywhere were overwhelming.

The cell phone traffic in Freedom, MT, back and forth from patients in the clinic to friends and family, was continuous. This caused many friends and family members to come to the clinic and try to enter to visit, which is customary. However, when they arrived at the clinic, they were greeted by the Army National Guard, keeping them from entering the clinic. All the Guard members would say was, "We are sorry, but we have orders to keep everyone out for their own safety."

This, of course, heightened everyone's concerns for their friends as well as themselves. Some then asked, "Are we in and danger here in Freedom?"

The Soldier responded, "We have been told that those outside the clinic are in no danger." While that helped some, the constant flow of concerned citizens continued, and the soldiers responded the same way.

Social media had crisis-exploded, and the Freedom Police Department was its unfortunate beneficiary. While most residents had followed the directive to stay home, panicked hundreds wanted to be "free" of Freedom. New nomads overstuffed their Ford F-150's, Chevy Suburban's, and Dodge Rams like Israelites heading to the desert, sputtering gas fumes and confusion. Over the fenders and roped to the roof racks, suitcases, ammo, coolers, furniture, and bedding made caravan to every town exit. Snake lines stuck behind National Guard blockades, military jeeps lassoing stray vehicles trying to go cross-country. Biological crisis was unsolved. Social media uncontrolled.

Chapter 15 – Freedom, Montana

Dr. Robinson was starting to feel the pressure. One hundred fifty-two patients were in their care, and some were beginning to fade with only IV's of saline and eyewashes to help irritation. The Army National Guard had arrived minutes after talking with Dr. Pace. Patients were scared and felt terrible, and all their caregivers looked like space travelers in their protective suits. It appeared to Cindy that they must have inhaled the ricin somehow as the patients did not present vomiting or severe vomiting and diarrhea. They did, however, present an extreme cough, which eventually contained blood, and in Father John's case, his lungs filled with fluid, and he couldn't breathe. Sister Deb had been at his side when he passed away and was still very distraught but helping.

Sister Deb stopped for a minute and confided in Dr. Robinson, "I am not doing well at all. You may have heard that I have a drinking problem, which is why I sometimes miss Masses on Sundays. I am so ashamed." Dr. Robinson hugged her and kept her close for a while, saying, "If you had been in church Sunday, like Father John, you would have been exposed to ricin, and you know the rest of the story. However, if Father John were here, he would be consoling everyone at the clinic. That, Sister Deb, would be your great act of kindness right now." Sister Deb thanked Dr. Robinson, wiped her tears away, and continued helping.

The Army National Guard presence was a godsend. Standing post around the clinic kept out the press and those that were friends of patients. In addition, they had placed ten large unmarked boxes outside the Center. When Cindy asked the Sergeant what they were for, he responded in a calm voice, "They are body bags, doctor."

Now Cindy was very anxious and could not wait for Dr. Pace to arrive. More patients were getting close to lung failure. It was about this time when her lack of sleep and adrenaline rush subsided, and Dr. Pace and his team suited up and came into the clinic.

She said loudly, "Dr. Pace – I am so glad you are here! We have plenty of medical help, but it doesn't seem to be doing more than keeping patients comfortable and, in most cases, not that comfortable."

One of the nurses interrupted Dr. Pace and Robinson to tell them that five more patients had expired - two children and three adults. The Sergeant had said to her that the Guard had a refrigerated truck on-site and would carry out any deceased victims and put them in bags and then into the truck, making sure they were properly identified. Two of his suited Privates were posted at the front of the Center and, when asked, would carry the deceased out and take care of everything. Cindy referred the nurse to one of the Privates and asked her to pass the word to the other caregivers on what to do.

Dr. Robinson spent the next thirty minutes bringing Dr. Pace up to the minute on the situation. Finally, he asked her, "Do you have everything under control here as my team and I need to go to the church and see if we can determine if the church was the source of the ricin and, if so – how it was used?"

"We are under control," she replied. "But losing patients quickly."

He added, "We have a communications expert that will handle all press releases as well as manage the media that has arrived and has set up outside. Instruct everyone that no one talks to the press except Betty Stevers, our expert. No one. And only you will talk with Betty, Cindy. This helps keep rumors or inaccurate information from spreading. We will have every news agency in the world here in no time flat."

"No problem, I understand. I will get that message to the staff, and thanks for taking that problem off my plate," Cindy replied.

"Is there anyone trustworthy who knows the church and can accompany us to the site," he hoped the answer was yes?

"Well – right over there is Sister Deb, who is a nun assigned to St. John's Catholic Church," Cindy replied, pointing to Sister Deb. "She is very distraught as she and Father John worked closely together, and she was with him when he died."

"Was she present during the Masses Sunday?" questioned Stan.

"No – she was not feeling good Sunday morning and had told Father John that she would not attend Masses," Cindy said. "I will introduce her to you," Cindy was walking toward Sister Deb as she was talking. Sister Deb was with Tommy, whose parents and sister had died. Tommy was close to death, and she was holding his hand. Minutes later, Tommy died, and Sister Deb kneeled and prayed. Oh, so young.

Sister Deb felt a tap on her shoulder and turned around to see Dr. Robinson and a man with her. Dr. Robinson introduced them to each other.

"Sister Deb," he said, "I am so sorry for your loss. I understand that you and Father John were close."

Sister Deb started crying and sat back down. She had seen more death in the last four hours than at any time in her life. Stan continued, "As you noticed and shared – all the people here are Catholic, and I need to have my team go to St. John's and do an investigation as to how these people all were exposed to ricin at the church. I need your help, Sister."

"I want to help," she said through her tears. Will I have to wear those plastic suits?"

"I'm afraid so, Sister," he helped her up. "You won't have to put it on until we go into the church." She followed him out the door and into the SUV.

When they arrived at the church, it was surrounded by yellow caution tape tied from tree to tree. Ten soldiers were standing post around the church. Stan showed the officer in charge his credentials, and they walked around the facility with the team paying close attention to the HVAC system against the rear of the church.

The HVAC expert looked closely at the system and said that the filters were on the other side of the wall. He had indicated earlier on the flight that particles would be in the filters if the ricin were airborne, which he would tag and bag for testing at the lab.

Sister Deb suited up and took the team through the rear entrance. The team split up, each with specific responsibilities. The team had to collect water, food, donuts, coffee, communion wafers, wine, holy water, daily bulletins, and anything else that the parishioners might have encountered from the time they entered the church to the time they left.

Dr. Pace had escorted the exhausted Sister to Father's office, where she might rest while the team did its work. *Don't leave me here, Doctor. This was Father's space. I can't stand it. Not now. Not yet. I know where he used to hide the Bailey's.* "Sister, is there anything else that Father or the altar boys used during or after the Masses on Sunday?"

"What do you expect? I was too hungover to go to Mass. That should have been me in that oxygen tent. The old, sot of a nun should be choking to death like the rest of them."

Stand grew impatient with her babble. "Sister, please concentrate. Was there anything about those Masses that was any different from the usual? Anything at all?"

"Well," she thought, "As we prepared for the celebration, Father was using a special green incense. The Pope required it as part of the World Peace Celebration. So, he would have placed the incense in the thurible to burn. It is right over there in a cabinet to the left against the wall on the altar."

Before Sister Deb could finish the sentence, Dr. Pace flew to the cabinet and spied the ornate thurible with chains lying in its usual top-shelf location. Stan's heart rate ticked faster—he could always tell. He motioned his assistant to remove and open it. Three white hooded suits anxiously hovered over the brass smoke thrower. What did they find? Remnants of burned incense that might just carry hope for the still-living Catholics at Freedom's Center.

"Get all of it—every last ash to the lab. Look for any leftover incense sticks." Stan ordered. "Incense and ricin—seems improbable, especially making it airborne—but must check with everything else. A terrorist brain lives in an improbable universe."

Stan wandered into the old sanctuary, and without realizing it, counted his way to row 12. His gaze moved upward, as do the eyes of many a sanctuary visitor. Marble-white plaster walls with black oaken trusses crisscrossing the nave were like arms embracing the simple nave over a barren altar. The Montana sun worked magic with the stained-glass Adoration of the Magi. Dog-eared hymnals and prayer books dropped cluttered the symbolic vista of Alfred Angel and Man's Journey from Humanity to Divinity. How many kneeling supplicants had these dust-crust arched walls seen? How many screeching babies, despaired widows, and lost souls?

Dr. Pace unexpectedly rolled himself into a Catholic boy of 10 again, sheepishly peeking at Mother Mary with guilt piles so high no confession could shovel. *I didn't mean to pull Rhoda Roberts pigtails—they were just stringy-hanging ropes that caught my hands. She really wasn't a witch face—I just liked it when her squinty eyes bugged out when I said "witch." Oh . . . and Rhoda's fat gut just got in the way of my wanna-be-a-man-fist, you know? It probably didn't hurt much. Bet she is some Catholic millionaire somewhere, building her own sanctuaries that are off-limits to snot-filled, name-calling little boys.* Stan had never asked Mother Mary for forgiveness or help, but Freedom, Montana might be the exception.

Stan's worn fingers clutched both pew and cell phone as he further pondered the Montana angle. Wasn't it full of white supremacy groups? What were their names? Sons of the South? New Order Rebs? He remembered old reports that some of these clan-klatches lived off the land and derided authority. Would a group like that target a church? The Center's ER wasn't full of African-Americans. Why Freedom, Montana, the other side of nowhere? Why just Catholics? Why now? Dr. Pace and his pew were soon parted. Goodbye, Rhoda pigtails. Hello, 50+ dead. Stan knew that it started in this place but would end somewhere else.

The CDC crew had spent over two hours in St. John's, filling vials and sample bags with every potential bit of evidence. Stan deployed his impatient-director voice, "Do we have everything we need so we can get the samples to a lab fast?" A half-dozen caps and scalps nodded affirmatively. Team techs would fly to the Seattle FBI Lab. "Expect results—two hours tops. Keep your white suits on— back to the Center's ER. Sister, let's go," Stan's words trailed behind him on their way out. No final kneeling. No extra prayers to the Virgin Mary. Just out—like dodging a reception poorly planned and ill-attended. Sister Deb did not look back.

The FBI's team had also arrived and were questioning everyone, including patients still living, townspeople, the police, businesses, and of course, all area residents with medical or chemistry backgrounds. Stan was hoping they uncovered something soon as every minute that went by would mean whoever was responsible for this attack was farther away. Canada was only a few hours' drive North from Freedom with no serious border checks.

"Ok, everyone," Stan announced. They had spent over two hours in the church. "Do we have everything we need so we can get the samples to a lab fast?" Everyone nodded, and they had plenty of bags to get to the jet. The team techs would fly to Seattle, where a terrific FBI Lab was located. Stan was hoping they would know more within hours of the testing.

Stan returned to the Health Center around 2:30 p.m. to find out that now 60 people had died. Now he was almost sure that the ricin had been airborne. The symptoms would concur. He guessed that all 153 would probably die by Tuesday sometime. He went into the conference room and called the President.

Dr. Pace locked the Center's conference room door and made a formal, confidential call to President Sutton. "Madame President, the CDC team has determined that parties unknown successfully completed an attack on members of the Catholic Church in Freedom, Montana. Attack mechanism: chemical agent ricin. Transfer method of agent to humans is yet unknown, but reasonable inference at this point is airborne—through incense, priest disbursed each Mass. Current dead: 60. Estimated casualties for all attendees at both Sunday Masses: 100% dead by Tuesday. FBI has arrived—investigations underway. Canada is only a few hours away—can't rule that out."

"How long on lab tests?" This was Carol Sutton's Paris, and she knew the cliffs from which she could fall quickly if Stan didn't get the roads cleared soon.

"Two hours," he replied. "Time for an official press release. Every major network is set up on the edge of Freedom, and while our communications expert is holding them off, it can't last. So far, the media can't get into town or to St. John's—the Guard has that tightened down. Unfortunately, a CNN videographer in a helicopter captured two headline-escalating scenes: the church wrapped around with yellow tape and Guard military hauling a black line of body bags from the Center. On social media by now—I haven't had time to check. Do you want me and my team to make the press release, or do you want your Press Secretary to do it from the White House?"

"Stan, as CDC Director, coming from you is protocol at this stage. Say that the White House has been informed. Make sure you indicate that this appears to be an isolated incident and that the FBI, working with local authorities, are investigating. If you trust the local doctor, a statement by Freedom's Health Center authorities would also help."

"Fine," Dr. Pace sighed simultaneous relief and dread—he knew what Carol's answer would be before he asked. "Will keep you posted. If the CDC could have prevented but missed the mark because of bad monitoring, political and professional hell would come. Be ready."

By 6:00 p.m. Tuesday, September 19th, the Army Guard's semi-truck contained 153 corpses—every Catholic who attended mass at St. John's on

Sunday, each body carefully tagged for its journey to the nearest Guard base for fast-track autopsies, hopefully no more than a week. What relatives, community, and media could not be told at this point—the government would have to incinerate all bodies at a secured facility. A decontamination team swarmed Freedom's Health Center when the front wheels of the Guard's semi, tailed by the CNN helicopter, crossed their own blockade on the west edge of town.

By 7:00 p.m., with blockades removed and multiple media outlets camped in across the street from Freedom's Heath Center, they and hundreds of town residents crowded the microphones corn-stalked on the Center's front steps. The Montana National Guard maintained its crowd-management presence, and its Commander and several Sergeants flanked the team at the podium.

"My name is Tim McLaughlin, FBI Agent. I can only share what we are doing as part of the investigation but cannot share specifics as the investigation is ongoing. Unfortunately, freedom has experienced a ricin attack at St. John's Catholic Church. We are currently casting a wide net looking at everyone with medical or chemical backgrounds that might have had a motive or means to perpetrate this attack. When we have more information, you will be brought up to speed. Now I would like to introduce Dr. Stan Pace, Director of the Center for Disease Control."

"I am going to give you an update as to what we know about the ricin attack. It appears to have been centered only in the local Freedom Catholic church, and it was administered in its deadliest airborne form. There is no antidote for ricin poisoning. Death by airborne ricin is almost certain in 24 to 48 hours. Along with the FBI, we will be investigating how the ricin was delivered, where it came from, by whom, and then go after the perpetrators. I want to introduce Dr. Cindy Robinson, Freedom Clinic head doctor."

"The past hours have been traumatic and beyond comprehension. Starting on Sunday afternoon, families began reporting to the clinic with the same symptoms. These were later deemed to be from ricin poisoning, as confirmed by the lab in Great Falls. We have lost 153 men, women, and children in Freedom from this attack. Doctors and staff followed protocol and kept patients as comfortable as humanly possible. Knowing there was no antidote heightened patients fears as you might expect."

Betty Stevers then stepped up to the microphone and asked for questions.

"Did the patients suffer?"

Dr. Robinson answered, "We kept patients as pain-free as possible, but suffocating is never without suffering."

"Were any of the health care workers taken ill?" Again Dr. Robinson responded, "No."

"Have there been any arrests or suspects identified?"

Tim answered, "Not at this time. It appears now that this was an isolated attack."

"What did the President say when she was informed?"

Stan answered, "President Cortney was very concerned and will be addressing the nation when more details are available. Her prayers are with all those that have died as well as family members not affected."

"How was the ricin transmitted?"

Stan again responded, "We do not know at this time. We have sent many samples from the church to the FBI Lab and are waiting for those results."

"Why was the Montana Army National Guard present?"

Tim responded, "We needed to contain the clinic and the church to protect the patients as well as the citizens. Therefore, the Governor approved the request as an emergency."

"Where was the deceased taken to?"

"Dr. Robinson answered," They have been taken to the Montana National Guard Headquarters where coroners are present and will do autopsies."

A few more questions were asked, but the final one would undoubtedly be the lead headline used by every news source, "Was this a terrorist attack?"

Tim answered the final question, "At this time, we do not know anything more than we have shared this evening. Jumping to conclusions without concrete facts will not help the investigation."

Betty took the microphone and announced that there would be an update at 8:00 a.m.PT and thanked everyone for their patience.

When it was over, the team went into the Center and sat down at the conference table. Stan said to Tim, "There were quite a few questions that we just don't have answers to yet. How hard is it going to be to track down whoever was responsible for the attack?"

"Before we discuss that, I need to call the President, and if it is ok with you three, I would like to put you on speakerphone so she can ask you any questions," he hoped this would be well received by the President.

The call was made, and the President was glad to have all four present. She said, "Please speak freely and tell me where we are at this point in the investigation?"

"Hello Madame, president, I am Tim McLaughlin, FBI agent in charge. The answer to that lies in the data," responded Tim. "As we investigate every little detail everywhere, it will eventually lead us to the perpetrator(s). The truth will be in the details. It always is. But whoever did this is long gone or was never here. We just don't know. The lab results will be critical and will be our next best lead. They knew what they were doing. But why Freedom? We need that answer, which will also point us in the right direction."

"Madame President, my name is Dr. Cindy Robinson, and I am the Chief of Staff for the Freedom Health Center. We have lost 153 people. Specifically, 46 children and 107 adults. Death due to airborne ricin is excruciating as the patient suffocates as their lungs fill up with fluid. We did everything we could. Unfortunately, there is no cure for ricin poisoning."

Betty Stevers introduced herself and stated, "Hello again, Madame President. We have held two press conferences and are thinking about one more in the morning to wrap it up here in Freedom. So I think from here on in, we need to switch to Washington D.C. for further updates if you agree."

"Susan," the President responded, "I agree. We have many more resources here and can control things better. Has the Governor been involved?"

"Yes, and he will be part of the press conference Wednesday morning," Betty answered.

"Fine," the President stated. "Stan, when are you returning to Atlanta or D.C.?"

"I plan to fly back Wednesday afternoon to D.C. as I need to meet with the FBI after the lab testing results are in. We will know a lot more at that point."

"Thank you for the update, everyone. I appreciate all you are doing for Freedom, Montana, and our country. We need to keep Americans well briefed without alarming them any further than they are already. We do not want what happened in Paris to happen here—ricin instead of bombs." All conference table eyes cross-locked at President Sutton's final sentence. No Paris here.

As Montana darkness swallowed the streets of Freedom, lives rearranged, and fears unknown swathed the middle-of-nowhere town that would be yesterday's news six months from now. "I don't know about anyone else, but I am totally shot," exclaimed Dr. Robinson. "Going home. You all have my cell number. See you in the morning." *Don't want them to see me cry. Have to maintain . . .Have to maintain . . . Wish Dr. Pace would stay around for a while.*

Everyone agreed to meet at 7:00 a.m. to sort out any new information and prepare for the press conference.

Sister Deb's favorite plaid, Lazy Boy, was soaked with nun tears. After several hours, she mustered to the bathroom. In the mirror, she saw a wrinkled face and double chin. Mouth wide open---but no sound. *Who is that? How can you cry with no sound? Glad they can't see me. Need Father John. Where's the Seagram's? He wouldn't want me to. Pour it down the sink.*

Agent McLaughlin and Dr. Pace went to a diner across the street from the worn but clean B&B in which they had been staying. The eatery was a postcard from Anywhere, USA: dark, narrow establishment with red, vinyl-covered swivel counter stools and two banks of grease-stained booths like dirty dentures in a cup. Tim and Stan walked quickly to the farthest, darkest table.

Stan forked-punched his hot beef sandwich in frustration. "What does your gut tell you? I respect your gut. It has gotten us out of some scrapes in the past."

"My gut is on the fritz, Stan," Tim answered. "Never seen this. We have only had about 22 ricin-involved cases from 1978 to 2015. Most of them were minor things like sending a scratch-and-sniff ricin letter to a girlfriend or ricin-laced letters sent to politicians. Most have been small or individual cases, nothing like Freedom."

"I was afraid of that. CDC's worst fear for real. We know how to react. We have protocol preventions for exporting and importing every known chemical that is dangerous or could be made dangerous. Every controlled substance is logged upon sale. This was one of our agenda items just a month ago for review. Maybe our monitoring lenses are too narrow . . ." Dr. Pace hadn't taken a breath.

"Shut up, Stan. God, take some valium or something," Tim cut off the rant before it got too loud and the fry cook overheard. "We can't anticipate everything. This is a first for me, and it is what I do for a living. I will remind you that whoever did this *only had to be right one time.* We must be right every time. You will surely hear that again. Remember, 9/11 is a good example. We are better at coordinating our agencies than we were then. Our agencies have stopped hundreds of attacks before they have taken place. You know we don't advertise what is working."

Dr. Pace knew he was right. "Tim, when do you think we will have all the lab results?"

Tim nearly choked on the last bites of a platter-sized tenderloin sandwich. "Stan, you know *it takes time* to test everything we sent to the lab appropriately. God Almighty! Where is your brain? You know the drill. They are working as fast as humanly possible. They will not sleep until the tests have been completed. Everything was sent as the highest priority. Finish that pile of gravy goop so we can go get some sleep."

One last gray gulp. "Thanks, man. Yes, sleep . . . that's it . . . just some sleep."

Chapter 16 – Aleppo, Syria-Thursday, September 21, 2017

Darcy had a new live-in boyfriend, Aazim, Syrian-born and Aleppo-raised. His name, according to him, meant "determined," and that and his strong ties in XTREM made him a perfect target for Darcy's plan, and XTREM had directed him to control and protect their new protégé—ideal pair. Aazim appeared to admire her direct style, would benefit within the XTREM community riding her ricin/green incense coattails, and certainly did not turn down the temporary opportunity for bedroom company. Darcy rarely thought of Steven, far away in a Berkeley lab completing a master's project in brilliantly planned blindness. Her time now focused on monitoring media communications and waiting for September 24, the Pope's Celebration of Peace Day. *Waiting*, she found, was a demanding companion.

On Thursday, September 21, the wait was over. Darcy heard "it" over the whistling teapot. *Must be a mistake. Not possible. Too early.* But a CNN voice announcer read the news blurb like scripture: "Breaking news. There has been a biological attack, likely ricin-related, at a St. John's Catholic Church in Freedom, Montana. 153 dead. The CDC and FBI underway lead a federal investigation. Suspects are unknown. Washington officials at the highest levels have made this a top priority. This incident has not been officially designated a terrorist attack at this time. More news to follow." Darcy reverse-snapped her slender neck just in time to see a helicopter-view shot of a church apparently jailed in yellow rope and then to military personnel carrying body bags to an unmarked truck outside what appeared to be a hospital.

Darcy's sharp eyes blinked, first back and then forth, from the screen to the iPad in her lap. Fast fingers fumbled from Twitter to Facebook to MSNBC and multiple secreted XTREM sites. Traditional media indicated that FBI and CDC officials did not know how the ricin was made airborne—tests were underway. *They will find ricin in the incense ashes and then back to the incense source, her old high school chum's beloved CNCS. They won't find anything. I should have got rid of her.* That oversight was now beyond correction.

Darcy rescued the screaming tea kettle, steeped some Chi, and marked her thinking with deliberate checks. That church used the green incense early. Pondering the why was a waste of energy. It was done. Not the large-scale of her hate dreams. What is the best scenario? Feds will conclude that the attack in Freedom was an isolated incident against that church—perhaps an individual once abused there or a Catholic-hater. One psychotic most likely swapped out the incense sticks at *only that church*—politically convenient conclusion by a rationally proper person. Unknown to the young victim turned terrorist: Dr. Stan Pace was neither politically correct nor rationally accurate.

Darcy's measured anxiety slobbered the lines she pondered *timing.* Could Feds complete the investigation before this coming Sunday, the 24th, when the rest of the 22,000,000 Catholics would inhale ricin at their Day of Peace Masses? Professor Pace's son would have to remember the "ricin" study he had agreed to, then trace back to students' names he had probably forgotten. What then?

Darcy clutched an Aazim-smelly comforter as she fell to the sofa, curled up, and played it out. Professor Pace would identify her, report that she had left peace Be with You

school. Through him, they would learn about Steven and their ricin project. *Steven will hold on about as long as it takes him to blink. Maybe he will lie about the Chicago facility to protect me. Why should he? Could have done better pretending with him. Another mistake left behind.* The Feds would locate her parents through school records—what a scene—then know she had fled to Syria—to grandparents, but not Aazim. *How many days will that take? Surely more than four—more than just four. . .*

Darcy crammed essentials into a backpack and texted Aazim to leave work now. XTREM would help her (or both) quickly disappear within its support network. She did not know how many hours it would take before her Berkeley picture ID would be mass-plastered on every social media site and globally most-wanted—a Berkeley PR disaster. So much planning—there was still time for her ricin debacle success—just a few days—that's all.

Aazim pressed a contact number on his phone, "Father, early performance went well. Need more quanuns." Aazim had learned the art of terse, coded communications in the XTREAM universe.

"How many?"

"Two—by end of day. More performances in four days." Aazim explained.

"Done."

"Thank you, Father."

"Anything for my Son."

Chapter 17 – Washington, D.C.

On that same Thursday in Washington, DC, the National Security Council had scheduled a meeting at 10:00 a.m. to hear a CDC status report regarding lab results from the samples gathered at St. John's in Freedom, Montana. Dr. Pace was ready.

At 9:00 p.m. the night before this meeting, Stan received a message that lab results were on their way to FBI Headquarters. Damn protocol. He was surprised to see Dr. Tim Matson, FBI's Division Administrator, waiting for him in a secured office by the time he got there. He and Matson went back many years, fought off political attacks, and argued about rules. While Stan dribbled the ball down the court to make an intelligent play, Matson rammed it down the nearest player's throat so he could go to lunch. The hate-respect relationship had always worked, though, and Stan expected no different this time.

"Been a while, Stan. Jesus, wandering around in the Montana wasteland— hell. Let's look at the bad news." Matson earnestly rubbed his club hands like a man ready for a rack of ribs, drooling and waiting for cardiac arrest.

"Every sample taken from *outside* the sanctuary was ricin-negative. Every sample from *inside* the sanctuary that was *covered*, for example, the extra communion wafers, tested negative. Every sample from *inside* the sanctuary that was *open to the air* tested ricin-positive. Conclusion: the ricing was airborne.

Thurible ashes tested ricing-positive, the only airborne source during mass that day. Conclusion: incense sticks tainted with ricin."

"Shit. How could an asshole get ricin in an incense stick?"

"Lab techs are working on multiple scenarios. May be many ways—don't know for sure. The Thurible storage cabinet wasn't locked. Anyone could have entered the church, dipped the sticks into a ricin solution, and put them back into place, and left unnoticed. Not like it's a high-security joint. Big, however—if the ricin was only a surface coating, it most like would not have survived the burning—not appearing, you see, in lab results."

"Agree," Stan struggled to visualize an angry jerk who just happened to have some ricin and just happened to be in Freedom, Montana. "If not surface coating, then what? Had to be mixed, yes? Some radicals in Montana who might know or find out how to do that—they hate the federal government."

"We are all over that in Montana," Matson felt the urge to ram a basketball. "FBI agents are interviewing every known person in Montana who has the means and connections to pull this off. Making ricin is not complex, so the ocean of possible Montanans might be bigger than you think."

Dr. Pace's stubble jaw turned itself uphill, pushing with it a short memory— something about ricin and father's students at Berkeley. *Can't remember exactly. Some study or other.* "I know. I know. I know," Stan echoed his impatience. "Need to find out where St. John's got the incense and interview."

"Hot damn! For once, we are ahead of all might Dr. Stan Pace," Tim chortled his win. "These guys all get their stuff from the same joint, the Chicago National Catholic Supplier, INC. Our agents are on a redeye as we speak. Those army flyboys can cough up rigs when we need them to. Getting damn fuckin' late, Stan. My ugly mug gets uglier when I'm tired. I get tired a lot, in case you haven't noticed."

"Slam dunk, ole' buddy," Stan grinned for the first time in days, albeit a butt-weary smile. "The NSC meets 10:00 a.m. tomorrow. Let me know ASAP if you find anything else between now and them. My phone is set on vibrate—I will watch for your call. While making ricin is easy, making it airborne through burning an incense stick would take more expertise than some hate-mongering clod off the Montana ranch would likely have. Narrows the field, eh? Thank your team for me. Order all agencies that connection between the incense sticks and the ricin attack is internal only. Repeat—internal only."

Chapter 18– Chicago - Chicago National Catholic Supplier, INC. / Glencoe

FBI Agents Jerry Oltrogge and Sandy Blau were waiting for the Chicago National Catholic Supplier, INC. (CNCS) to open at 7:30 a.m. It was a beautiful, partly cloudy, and humid day in the Chicago north loop area, which was pretty standard for the Windy City in September. Just to be on the legal side of everything, they had secured search warrants in case they were needed. The warrants were for computers, materials, paperwork, files, orders forms, and anything else related to the incense sticks sold to St. John's Catholic Church in Freedom, Montana. Just in case, Jerry had added and any other orders for incense sticks sold by CNCS. Unfortunately, the news of how the ricin was made airborne in Freedom was not yet public knowledge.

The receptionist welcomed the agents and buzzed Betty Wilcox. Ms. Betty Wilcox, manager, and Mr. Charles Gilson greeted the agents in the lobby, introductions were exchanged, and Betty asked the agents to come back into their conference room. "So what is this all about," Betty sternly requested.

Agent Oltrogge replied, "We have a situation that you have probably seen on the news regarding the ricin attack in Freedom, Montana."

Betty quickly said, almost shouting, "That was so terrible – I just couldn't tear myself away from the coverage. So many deaths. So sad. What does that have to do with CNCS?"

Seeing that Wilcox was quite defensive, Agent Blau pulled out the search warrant, handed it to Wilcox, and said, "Here is a search warrant allowing us to look at your orders, products, production, computers, and anything else associated with the production, sale, and distribution of incense sticks to Freedom, Montana or any other buyers."

Sitting back and crossing her arms across her chest, Betty was almost faint, and most of the blood had rushed away from her face. "Well – she said. We distributed up to four sticks to every Catholic church in the United States on September 1st for use on September 24th for World Catholic Peace Day. That would number about 22,000 sticks to over 17,000 Catholic churches. You still haven't said why you want to look at all the information contained in the warrant? Do we need our corporate attorney or…"

Charles Gibson interrupted Betty seeing that she was about to lose it, introduced himself as the Production Manager, and said, "Is there some connection with our product and the ricin attack in Freedom?"

"Well, we are exploring every avenue, Mr. Gibson," answered Agent Oltrogge. "Do you have any incense sticks left in inventory that were not distributed or held back for additional orders?"

"Actually, we do," replied Charles. "I guess we have about 250 or so in the warehouse. I can get them for you if you wish?" Charles was also getting more than a little concerned.

Charles left with Agent Blau while Agent Oltrogge stayed with Ms. Wilcox. "Please understand, Ms. Wilcox, that we are covering all our bases, trying to determine how this tragedy happened. The FBI lab has confirmed that the ricin was made airborne via incense sticks. So, we must examine them and determine if the ricin infusion took place at your facility or after delivery."

Betty finally uncrossed her arms and leaned forward, and said, "We tested those incense sticks before distribution, and we are all still very much alive. So, there is no way ricin was infused at our facility. No way." She leaned back and crossed her arms again.

Charles and Agent Blau returned with about 250 incense sticks in a sealed bag, and the green-tinted sticks were also individually sealed within the bag. "Before we rush to any judgment," announced Agent Oltrogge, "let's take these sticks to our lab here in Chicago where we have what's called a simple, accurate, and highly sensitive test to detect and quantify ricin. Not all labs have this, but we are fortunate to have one here in Chicago. Agent Blau, why don't you take these to the lab, drop them off, and come on back while we continue talking. Have the lab call me as soon as the results are in, which should take about 30 minutes."

Agent Blau got up, took the bag, and left. The FBI lab was only 10 minutes away, so she would probably return at about the same time Jerry would get the call. She was surprised that he wanted to stay back, but he was the senior agent, and she followed his orders.

"So tell me about the testing of these incense sticks?" asked Agent Oltrogge. "How many sticks were tested and by whom."

Charles responded, "We were excited to receive the bid for this order, which netted CNCS over $330,000. So, after the initial batch of 300 was produced, six of us ceremonially lit a stick and watched it burn until it was out to make sure they worked as expected. None of us became sick or ill, if that is what you are asking. They all burned as expected!"

"That really helps Mr. Gilson," said Agent Oltrogge. "Can you go through with me the production process, and please use names for everyone that worked with the production as you explain it to me."

Agent Oltrogge took out his recorder and a notepad from his briefcase and took down all the information shared by Charles. It was very detailed, and clearly, he had a good handle on every aspect of the production process. At this point, Agent Blau returned from the lab, and about 10 minutes later, the call came into Agent Oltrogge, indicating that the sticks were clean with no traces of ricin.

"Well – good news. The lab says the incense sticks we just dropped off were clean with no traces of ricin. Could we visit with the six of you that were part of the production and that lit the initial batch?" Asked Agent Oltrogge.

"Sure," announced Charles, and he left to get the employees on his team.

Betty was now much more relaxed and able to think clearer. "I am relieved that our product did not cause the deaths in Freedom. You have no idea how relieved. This would have been catastrophic for us." She wished she could excuse herself for a moment to take a Xanax as she was working towards a panic attack.

Charles entered the room with the four workers, and they began to go over in detail what each had done in the production process leading up to the test batch and the manufacturing of the additional 22,000 incense sticks. It was almost a mirror of what Charles had previously shared with the agents.

"Has anything happened recently with your business or employees that was unusual or out of the ordinary? Anything come to mind at all?" probed Agent Blau.

They all thought for a while, and then Betty shared, "Really – the only unusual thing that has taken place was a homeless man was killed in our parking lot a while back. Nothing like that has ever happened around here, but that didn't have anything to do with our business. The Chicago police interviewed our folks, and none of us had ever seen this man or knew him. We don't know what the outcome of that investigation was, and we didn't expect to be told as there were no ties between the man and our employees."

The rest of the team couldn't think of anything else. Things were actually pretty much business-as-usual.

"Thank you so much for your cooperation, "Agent Oltrogge stated. "we will be in touch with any further developments regarding the incense sticks. Also, we may want to have our lab technicians go through your production equipment. I will let you know. Here is my card. Please call if anything else comes to mind."

Agent Blau also thanked the team for their time, asked that records of orders and the production schedule be forwarded to his office, and handed out his card to everyone.

They left the business, walked to their car, and Agent Blau commented to his partner, "Well – that was a bust. I doubt that the homeless man's murder was associated with CNCS, or the police would have dug more deeply into the business looking for any ties. Let's check with whoever caught the case with the Chicago PD and see what they have, just in case."

Jerry said to Sandy, "You drive – I have to call Tim in D.C. Tim McLaughlin answered his cell phone, and Jerry explained that the leftover incense sticks at the plant tested perfectly normal with no traces of ricin.

They drove back to their Chicago office, contacted homicide, got the detective's name that caught the case and asked to have him call regarding this specific case and that it was very important. Within fifteen minutes, the detective called and asked the FBI agents if they could come to his office as he was swamped. They agreed and drove over.

Detective Cory Marshall was a middle-aged man that had been on the force since he was twenty-one. He was a seasoned detective with an excellent track record for solving homicides. He welcomed the agents, and they went to an unused interrogation room and sat down.

Detective Marshall started, "So, as you may know, Chicago experienced 762 murders last year, which is about 15 murders a week. It is tough to keep up with this heavy load, but we sure try." He opened the file on the homeless man that was murdered in the CNCS parking lot.

He continued, "He was knifed twice, and the coroner indicates that there was no hesitation to either of the stab wounds. Therefore, whoever killed him was serious. So, why does the FBI have an interest in this homicide?"

Agent Blau explained, "We are looking into all aspects of the ricin attack in Freedom, Montana, and it appears that the incense used during their two masses was contaminated with ricin. The company that manufactured these special incense sticks is CNCS, and we are just making sure that this murder had nothing to do with any part of CNCS."

"Well," detective Marshall sat up and said, "We believe there is no connection with anyone at CNCS and that probably the poor old fellow was in the wrong place at the wrong time. Either a street gang doing an initiation or another homeless person wanting something that the old man had probably was what happened."

He continued, "I know it sounds like we are just excepting that Chicago will just have a lot of murders, but that isn't our feeling. After 2003, we installed over 25,000 cameras, which are still in operation today. Clearly, more of them are in high crime areas than others, and the criminals are aware that they might be being watched. We checked the cameras close to CNCS and found nothing helpful the night of this homicide."

Agent Blau asked if any of these cameras might have been in a place that picked up any cars driving by or out of the CNCS parking lot that night.

He quickly responded, "We weren't that lucky. The closest camera was not facing the parking lot and only was recording street traffic at the intersection a block away from CNCS. So nothing there was helpful."

"How long are the recordings kept?" Agent Oltrogge asked.

"Great question," he quipped, "90 days unless there is a reason not to allow the recording to erase at day 91 automatically, so there is always 90 days on hand for any camera. The recordings are all automatically transmitted to the Chicago Crime Prevention and Information Center. A team monitors cameras and can manually control any camera when they detect unusual happenings."

Agent Oltrogge continued, "So if we wanted to look at the recording from that night at that intersection, that would be possible?"

"Sure – no problem. We work with other agencies like the fire department and DCI and have previously cooperated with the FBI. Let me get you the number you can call and set up a session. Could probably go there today if you wanted," he retrieved the number, gave it to the agents, and wished them well. They shook hands, and the FBI agents left on their way to the Information Center located at 3510 S. Michigan, 4th floor.

Agent Oltrogge commented to Agent Blau on the short drive, "Everyone thinks the FBI is a glamorous job with tons of action like in all the movies. They don't cover what we're are about to do, which is look at hours of footage, running visible license plates and probably getting nothing for hours of work!"

"Yep – you are so right!"

Chapter 19 – UCB – Professor Pace's Office

"Dad – sorry I took so long responding to your text about the master's project presentation. So why is there only one student making the presentation?" Stan's cell phone seemed slippery, so he changed ears.

"Hey – great to hear your voice, son. I'm not sure. The young man on the project indicated that his project partner dropped out of school to his surprise, as well. But stranger things have happened with college students. It looks like you have your hands full up there in Freedom."

Stan's grip tightened as he responded, "That is an understatement, dad. I have no clue how the burning incense used in the masses released ricin without destroying its destructive properties with the high heat. We have never seen this."

"Interesting," the professor pondered. "I agree that this is unusual and very crafty. Whoever did this had to have a pretty good knowledge of chemistry and the ability to create a formula that would make the ricin airborne in the smoke in its most dangerous form. The ricin had to have been mixed with more than incense to protect it. I'm at a loss right now to figure it out, but give me some time, and I will get back to you."

"Thanks, dad – I'm swamped now, and tell the young man that I will get back to you when I get this situation under control. I'm sure he will understand."

"No problem Stan," his dad was always his supporter. "I'll call you if I get some ideas regarding the incense." With that, they both hung up.

Stan sat back and pondered. Thursday, and still no clue how this happened or by whom.

Chapter 20 – Chicago, FBI and Video Surveillance

Agent Blau and Oltrogge reviewed all the video footage at the intersection right by the CNCS company during the hour before and the hour after the coroner's report indicated that the homeless man had been killed. Car after car went through this intersection, and they had to zoom in to get the license plates if they were visible. Then, when they were finished, they entered all the license plate numbers into the computer to identify the owners.

This exercise produced 62 names ranging from the suburbs to the city proper. However, they still had no clue if any of these names would be associated with killing the homeless man. So their next step was to run the names through VICAP to see if any of the names were associated with people with criminal records. A few had some arrests, the rest only some parking tickets.

They went back to the Chicago FBI office and gave 12 agents each about six names to start contacting and asking them if they remember anything suspicious on the night in question. This was a long shot for sure, but it was necessary.

After an hour, one of the agents motioned to Agent Blau to come over to her desk. "I just called a Marsha Oban living in Glencoe, and she said that her daughter, Darcy, used their car on that date but knew nothing else. When I asked her if I could speak with Darcy, she said she had left to visit her grandparents in Syria and continue her education in Aleppo. I don't know if this is anything, but I wanted to pass it along to you." Agent Blau thanked the rookie agent and motioned for Jerry to come to her desk. She explained what the agent had told her and asked what Jerry thought.

The agents ran Darcy Oban's name through the system and found nothing. Not even a parking ticket. She was a biochemistry student at the University of California at Berkley. Nothing unusual.

"Interesting and probably worth a call to Washington. If we don't, and it later becomes important, we will look like fools and lose our jobs. Always error on the side of caution. Call it in," agent Oltrogge smiled!

Sandy picked up the phone and relayed the information to headquarters, where everything surrounding the Freedom attack was being logged in. Within 15 minutes, a call came back from Tim McLaughlin, the lead agent in the investigation.

"Hey – you might have stumbled onto something. This may be nothing but drive up to Glencoe and visit with her parents and find out everything you can about Darcy Oban."

Both agents went directly to their car and headed up to Glencoe.

Chapter 21 – Washington, D.C.

Stan received that call from Tim briefing him with the meeting at CNCS. Now Stan was getting worried that there were just no leads in this terrible case. He had to get over to the White House for the NSC meeting. On his way, he called Sister Deb in Freedom.

"Sister Deb," he greeted, "This is Dr. Pace. How are you doing?"

"She replied, "Thank you so much for calling Dr. Pace. I'm trying to get my head around what just happened to our community. We have so many funerals to plan and grieving relatives to help. It almost is too much for me. But that isn't really why you called, was it, Dr. Pace?"

"You have a way of getting right to the point, Sister," he responded. "Tell me, why did St. Johns celebrate Catholic World Peace Day a week before the rest of the world?"

"Well, Father John's brother was getting married out East on September 23rd, and he was officiating the ceremony. He asked our parish council if we could celebrate a week early so he could be at his brother's wedding ceremony as he had promised him a year earlier that he would officiate. The council was perfectly happy to move it up a week. Why do you ask?' Sister Deb curiously questioned.

"I can't answer that right now, Sister, but I will when I have a better grasp of the entire situation. I promise I will call you back when I know more. You take care of yourself, Sister Deb," he hung up.

The car service dropped him off at the White House, and he went directly to the Oval Office, hoping that he could brief the President before the NSC meeting. Her assistant called the President, and she asked Stan to come in.

"Madame President," she could tell that something was wrong as I almost ran into the office. "I will be receiving a call from Tim at the FBI, and we may be looking at one of the worst potential terrorist attacks on America in history. We will know within the hour. The ricin attack in Freedom, Montana, while terrible, may have saved the lives of millions of Catholics if what we think is accurate. We know the ricin was airborne utilizing incense sticks burned during the Masses at Freedom. They celebrated a week early so the local priest could officiate his brother's wedding this coming Saturday."

"Are you saying that every Catholic Church in the nation may have these contaminated incense sticks in their possession right now?" The President was flushed as she spoke. "Oh my God….and sat down….."

Stan interrupted her, "We will know during the NSC meeting, Madame President. I did not want to spring this on you in that meeting. I will receive the call after some testing of sticks taken from a Washington D. C. Catholic Church. If that tests positive, we have a threat that can be stopped but clearly will panic the nation as we will only have Saturday to accomplish everything."

"The door to the oval office opened, and the President's Assistant said, "You have an NCS meeting in five minutes Madame President," and closed the door.

"Ok, Stan," the President had her hand on her chin in thought, "We will start the meeting with the scheduled agenda, and you have my permission to interrupt after you get the call and go over everything regardless of the test results. This is all happening so fast, Stan."

She had called Stan by his first name, which she usually never did in the Oval office. He knew she was terribly concerned, as was he. They walked together to the NSC meeting and sat down.

The Director of National Intelligence, Matt Harvey, started the meeting with a briefing of communication chatter and reports of potential terrorist plans in Europe. He explained that all agencies in every country were communicating every hour with any information, primarily referring to Freedom, Montana. He continued explaining that the FBI was interviewing many Montana militants and extremists but that nothing of any substance had been uncovered.

"No one is taking credit for this attack, and we are concerned as that could mean it was not XTREM or other groups that are responsible. Usually, after five days, someone comes forward, boasting about their feats of terror," Matt sighed as he put down his paperwork. "This silence is concerning."

Stan's phone vibrated, and he excused himself. "Tim – what do you have?" He asked.

"Well – this is either your worst nightmare or the luckiest catch we have ever made. It depends on how you view this. The sticks from St. Peter's Catholic Church on Capitol Hill tested positive for ricin. So today is Saturday, and hopefully, the rest of the nation's over 17,000 US Catholic Churches aren't going to celebrate Peace Day early as they did in Freedom prematurely." Tim was out of breath. "We are pulling the sticks from ten more cities to test just to make sure it is nationwide."

"Thanks, Tim – I will call you back with our next steps. Hold tight for now." He went right back into the NSC meeting. Matt was still giving his report when he interrupted.

"Excuse the interruption, Matt, but we have a situation. The FBI CD Lab has confirmed an excellent chance that ricin-infused incense sticks are present at every Catholic Church in the United States. They are to be used this Sunday, tomorrow, for Catholic World Peace Day. The incense sticks at St. Peters on Capitol Hill just tested positive, and ten more cities will be tested within the hour. The FBI has a lead they are pursuing that may or may not be worth anything. But more importantly, we are on a very tight timeline to get the incense sticks collected before Sunday's Masses."

"My God," President Sutton uttered. "We must hold a National Press Conference quickly before the rumor mill gets to the media, and they write their own version."

Matt jumped in, "Madame President. Unfortunately, there aren't enough FBI agents in the country to go to every Catholic Church and pick up these incense sticks. But there are police in every city and county in the nation that can accomplish this quickly and hopefully in one day. So holding a press conference is a wise move, but we first need to get to the local police officials everywhere on when and how to pick up these incense sticks. Is there any danger in handling them?"

Stan quickly answered, "As long as they are in the plastic wrapping they were delivered in, there is no cause for alarm. I would have the officers bring zip-lock evidence baggies and place them in these just to be safe. The CDC is part of the National Disaster Preparedness, Response, and Recovery Network, which every country is part of. They have a plan for this exact situation. Our agency will gladly put the protocol notice out to every county right before the press conference is held."

"Perfect, Stan," Matt responded. "But we need to develop talking points for the press conference. What is the status of the investigation?"

Again, Stan answered, "The FBI has a lead that they are pursuing in a Chicago suburb. That is the only firm lead they have at this time."

The President jumped in, "I need the talking points developed quickly. Dr. Pace will be with me as well as Director Harvey and Press Secretary Robinson. This will give the country the understanding that the situation is well in hand, especially coming from Directors and not just my office. We will take questions that I know aren't everyone's favorite venue, but it is essential for full transparency. So, let's get started."

Stan reminded the President on the way back to the Oval Office that communications were essential to keep the country from panic. He remembered what the CDC manual mentioned and tried to quote it, remembering, "**Effective communication with the public through the news media will also be essential to limit terrorists' ability to induce public panic and disrupt daily life.**" She nodded.

Chapter 22 – Glencoe, Illinois

Before Jerry and Sandy had gotten far, an urgent call from Washington came through. Things had changed substantially, and millions were in potential danger. They were to return to the company that produced the incense sticks, interview everyone, and ask only one question, "Do any of you know Darcy Oban? If any of them do, question them about recent communications or meetings."

They turned around and went straight to the company. They entered and asked the receptionist to have Betty Wilcox come up so they could talk and said it was an emergency.

Betty came up quickly, and the agents said that they needed her to get all the employees together to ask one straightforward question. She agreed, and they headed for the conference room. After everyone was present, Agent Blau asked, "Does anyone here know Darcy Oban?"

Everyone looked at each other, shrugging except for Nancy Martens, who said, "Yes – she is a friend, and we went to high school together." They excused the rest of the employees and sat down with Nancy.

"When was the last time you communicated with Darcy," Agent Blau was direct.

"We kind of just ran into each other this summer and had lunch together just a few months or so ago. So why are you asking?"

Agent Oltrogge didn't answer her question but asked another. "Would she have had any access to CNCS, or did you let her into CNCS at any time?"

Nancy was now very nervous, "Of course not. I gave her a tour, and she helped me with some marketing ideas with the Sun Times, and that was about it."

"So, nothing unusual or out of the ordinary?"

"No – nothing," she was now shaking a little.

"Do you carry your work keys in your purse?" Agent Blau continued.

"Why, yes!"

"Was there ever a time when you left your purse with her for any reason?"

Nancy thought for a while and then shared, "Only one time when we were at lunch, and I used the restroom. I took my purse with me but left my keys on the table. They were there when I returned."

"Nancy, if you think of anything else, please give me a call, and thanks for your time." Agent Blau handed her a card, and they all got up.

Nancy asked, "So what is wrong here, and why all the questions?"

"There may be a time when we can share that, Nancy, but now is not that time," and the agents left for Glencoe. On the way, they relayed the information from the interview and confirmed that one employee did know Darcy Oban. In their opinion, Darcy used the past friendship to gain access to the company potentially.

The drive from CNCS to Glencoe on the outer drive seemed to take forever as FBI Agents Jerry Oltrogge and Sandy Blau needed to find answers quickly. Finally, they pulled up to an enormous old home overlooking Lake Michigan. The circular drive was well-manicured and could have been on the cover of Better Homes and Gardens. They got out of the car and rang the doorbell to the right of the beautiful massive wooden door.

The door opened, and a beautifully dressed woman answered. FBI Agents Jerry Oltrogge and Sandy Blau showed Mrs. Marsha Oban their credentials and asked if they could come in and speak to her and her husband.

"My husband, Faraz, is at work," she said. "Please come in. How can I help you?"

"We need to speak with you about your daughter, Darcy," agent Oltrogge explained.

Mrs. Oban lowered her head a little, starred at the floor, and said, "Darcy had visited her grandparents in Aleppo, Syria in August, and decided to transfer from UCB to the University of Aleppo to finish her Master's Degree. We were distraught as UCB is one of the best universities in the world, but we were also excited that she was going to spend time with my husband's parents." Both agents already knew what her answer would be.

"Does Darcy have a cell number or a number where we can reach her?" Agent Blau asked.

"I noticed as I was cleaning her room after she left that her cell phone was in her desk drawer. When I talked to her at her grandparent's home in Syria, she said that it was too expensive to use the cell in Syria. I have her grandparent's phone if that will help. But what is so urgent, and should I call my husband to come home?" Mrs. Oban sounded somewhat frantic.

"Besides her cell phone, did Darcy have a laptop or desktop computer?" Agent Oltrogge ignored her question for the time being.

"Yes, but she took her laptop computer with her to use at the university," replied Mrs. Oban very anxiously. "Tell me why you need to speak to her?"

"We are not trying to alarm you, Mrs. Oban, but it is an urgent case of national security that she might have information to help us," explained Agent Oltrogge. "Could we have her cell phone and have the grandparent's number in Aleppo." She gave them the number 011-21-555-1212. "Do her grandparents speak English, Mrs. Oban?"

She anxiously answered, "Yes, they do." She added, "I think I need my husband here for the rest of this conversation," Mrs. Oban stated. "He is only 15 minutes away." She picked up her cell phone and dialed Faraz and asked him to please come home, and told him that the FBI was asking questions about Darcy.

Agent Blau visited with Mrs. Oban while Agent Oltrogge called his office, explaining the interview status. His supervisor indicated that two additional agents were driving up a search warrant. The warrant was for all computers in the home, cell phones, work products from CNCS, and any other information or data containing the word ricin, castor beans, or Freedom. If anything were suspicious, the forensics team would be tasked to the home for a complete search.

Mr. Oban and the two additional FBI agents arrived about the same time. Mr. Oban let the agents into the home, and one of the agents handed Agent Oltrogge the search warrant. Agent Oltrogge introduced the other three agents to Mr. Oban, and they all sat down in the living room.

Agent Oltrogge started, "Let me be very specific, Mr. and Mrs. Oban. The incident in Freedom, Montana, causing 153 deaths, has been traced back to CNCS incense sticks used at their Masses last Sunday. As will be reported, these sticks contained ricin, which was determined to be the cause of these deaths. Your daughter Darcy may have been involved with the incident or may have valuable information to help in the investigation."

Both parents looked at each other, and Mr. Oban stated, "You can't believe that Darcy had anything to do with the attack in Freedom, Montana. That's insane. She is a straight 'A' student at UCB, has never been in any trouble, and would never be involved in anything like you are suggesting. Are you targeting her because she looks like a Muslim?"

"No, sir," answered Agent Blau, "We need to speak to her, and it is urgent."

"I gave them your parent's phone number Faraz," Mrs. Oban interjected.

Mr. Oban stood and said, "Then you can contact her there, and you will see that she knows nothing."

"Does she have any friends that she was close to at UCB that we might visit with," asked Agent Oltrogge, hoping to calm down Mr. Oban?

Mr. Oban looked at his wife and said," She would know more about that than I do, but unless you have a warrant, we would like you all to leave now."

At this point, Agent Oltrogge knew things were going to get tense, and he didn't miss a beat, "Here is your warrant Mr. Oban. We will be looking through the home for the items listed and will be taking them with us. Please remain here in the living room with Agent Blau while we execute the warrant. This is a matter of National Security." With all his previous experience, Agent Oltrogge believed that Darcy's mother and father did not know of Darcy's involvement, if any, in the ricin infusion at CNCS.

Mr. Oban called his attorney and explained what was going on. He advised them to allow the agents to carry out the warrant and not interfere and asked him to copy the warrant and email it to him. Finally, he advised them both not to talk any further with the agents unless he was present.

About an hour later, the Agents were finished and had taken numerous bags out of the house. Agent Oltrogge asked both parents if they had cell phones, and it so, he needed them. Mrs. Oban said, "Yes – but that's not fair. What are we going to use? How will we contact people or be contacted?"

"I'm sorry for the inconvenience," replied Agent Blau, "But you will get them back. We need to check out everything." She was thinking that Darcy may have used her parent's phones without them knowing it. Both parents begrudgingly gave them their phones, knowing they still had a seldom-used land line to use if needed.

As soon as Agent Oltrogge got into the car, he dialed the grandparent's number in Syria, knowing it was late in the evening with the time difference of eight hours later. A quiet voice answered in Arabic and said that Agent Oltrogge took as hello.

"Am I speaking to Mrs. Oban, grandmother of Darcy Oban.? He asked.

She quickly switched to English and said, "Yes. Who is this?"

"My name is FBI Agent Jerry Oltrogge in Chicago, and I need to speak with Darcy. Marsha said it was ok to call you. Is Darcy there, please?"

"What is this about?" she questioned.

"We believe that she can help us with an investigation we are working on," he knew she could do more than help them!

"Well," paused the grandmother, "She was only here for a few weeks and has since moved into an apartment with a friend. I don't have a phone number for her, and we have been a little worried that she hasn't called us since she moved out."

"Thank you so much for your cooperation, Mrs. Oban. I will call you back if I need anything else. Do you have anything handy to write down my phone number?" She said yes, and Jerry gave her his phone number and asked that if

Darcy made contact, please give her his number and ask her to call. Of course, Jerry knew full well that Darcy would never call him.

On the ride back to their Chicago offices, Jerry called Tim and brought him up to speed with the interview with Darcy's parents and the conversation with the grandmother in Aleppo, Syria.

"Get ready, Jerry," Tim explained, "There is going to be a press conference to end all press conferences in about fifteen minutes. So if anyone calls your office, go into the Shultz mode and refer them to me! Let me know what you get from everything you took from the Oban house ASAP."

Chapter 23 – Washington D.C. – White House

News release: President Cortney Sutton - Matt Harvey, Director of National Intelligence – Dr. Stan pace, Director of the Center for Disease Control, will be addressing the nation in thirty minutes from the White House briefing room with an update on the ricin poisoning attack in Freedom, Montana. After statements, questions from the press will be taken.

The nation paused and waited for more news about what had happened in Freedom, MT. Every television network, streaming system, laptop, cell phone, radio, and college classroom was tuned into the press, discussing what they felt may or may not be addressed. The nation was more than frightened. Elderly folks hadn't seen anything like this since JFK was assassinated.

In the Oval Office, President Sutton reviewed her address. Stan listened to it along with Matt Harvey and Denise Robinson. They agreed that it was perfect. Matt then said, "Next, I will be bringing the country up to speed on the investigation." Stan said he would go last, explaining how the ricin was made airborne and how we think the threat has been thwarted.

"Does this sound ok," Stan asked?

The White House Press Secretary, Denise Robinson, was with us as she was terrific at giving good and bad news to the press who loved her. "It all sounds good. I will caution each of you that if you get a question that you don't have an answer to or don't want to answer, you will get back to them later with that information. Don't worry about remembering as it is all being recorded for later playback."

The president said, "Ok, let's go."

They walked to the Briefing Room, and Denise Robinson stepped up to the podium with the blue and white presidential crest behind her and said, "Good afternoon, everyone. I want you to know that you will be hearing from the President, The Director of National Intelligence, and the Director of the Center for Disease Control in that order. We will ask you to hold all your questions until all three have finished their statements. At that time, I will direct questions to the appropriate person. Ladies and gentleman of the press and the Nation, The President of the United States."

Everyone stood up for President Sutton, and she started, "Please be seated. As you all know, we have experienced a terrible loss of 153 men, women, and children in a ricin attack in Freedom, Montana. That investigation, as you will hear from Director Harvey, is ongoing. He will bring you up to the minute on that status. The next part of this terrible story is very frightening but has been contained. While 153 Catholic souls have been taken in Freedom, that incident may have saved millions of the over 72 million Catholics in our nation that may have attended World Peace Celebrations Sunday."

She continued, "Father John Warner, Catholic priest in Freedom, asked his Parish Council if they would allow him to celebrate Catholic World Peace Day a week earlier so he could officiate his brother's wedding this coming Saturday. They agreed, and the Masses were held last Sunday. You all know the results from that terrible day."

"We have learned that all the special green incense sticks to be used during the Peace-Be-with-You portion of the Masses in every Catholic Church on the World Peace Day in the United States were infused with the poison ricin, produced and distributed by the Chicago National Catholic Supplier, INC. in Chicago. They currently are being confiscated from every Catholic Church in our Nation as I speak. We believe, at this point, the Chicago-based company did not know that their product had been tampered with. Had Freedom not celebrated a week early, our Nation would have experienced a worse and devastating disaster."

"The next two speakers will detail where we are at this point. No one has taken responsibility for the Freedom attack. Obviously, because they were hoping we would not find out the rest of the story in time. Rest assured, America, we will not rest until the person or persons or groups responsible for this attack on our country are brought to justice or eliminated. Now I would like Director Harvey to speak."

Matt stepped up to the podium. "I want to assure all Americans that the investigation by the FBI and the CDC agency is well underway. We cannot give you any exact information as we do not want to give the perpetrators/terrorists any advanced warnings about what we are looking at. We have an excellent lead. It does not include any Montana extremists or militants, as was previously hypothesized by the press. The threat to Catholics at their Masses this coming Sunday has hopefully been eradicated as

I speak. You can go to church without fear. I would like to introduce Dr. Stan Pace, Director of the Center for Disease Control."

Stan moved up to the podium and started, "Thanks to you, Madame President and Director Harvey. I have seen some of the press in Freedom, Montana, and thank you for making that long journey to cover this terrible tragedy. Airborne ricin is hard to manufacture. Only someone with very skilled training could have pulled this off. When ricin is airborne, it is deadly, and there is no antidote. As was the case in Freedom, 153 people died within 48 hours of exposure."

"Currently, the National Disaster Preparedness, Response, and Recovery Network have been activated. Every county in our nation participates in this network. As we speak, police in every community are rushing to all Catholic Churches today, Saturday, and recovering the ricin-infused incense sticks. They are in no danger of exposure, and the American public is now in no danger of exposure. I appreciate everything the CDC teams have done to react to this tragedy."

He stepped back, and Denise Robinson moved to the podium and asked for questions. Everyone had their hand up and wanted their question answered on air. Denise picked first the NBC reporter who asked, "How did you determine that the ricin-infused incense sticks were in every Catholic Church in the USA?"

Denise asked Matt to take the question. "We first determined how the ricin was made airborne in Freedom which was burning the incense sticks, and then went to the Chicago Company that produced and distributed the incense sticks. We found that the extra non-distributed sticks were not contaminated, which led us to believe that the contamination occurred after the initial test batch was produced. The FBI then, making sure that Freedom was the only target, went to another Catholic Church in a major city and found that their incense sticks were also contaminated. Then ten Catholic Churches were contacted in major cities, and their incense sticks were also tested. They were all positive for ricin. We were on a tight timetable. We only had one day to determine everything I just shared, or tens of millions would have died. Most certainly, that was the person(s) or terrorist's goal."

Denise then said, "Next question CNN. Yes – Dr. Pace – How could someone get ahold of this much ricin without detection?"

Stan again stepped up to the podium, "That is an excellent question and has been a well-documented and published fear of the CDC for a long time. We are vulnerable to a chemical attack. It is easier than it seems. I will not give you a lesson on making ricin, but it is not simple to get castor beans. If you can, it is easy to follow a process then to make ricin. Only a very skilled person or persons could make ricin airborne, which happened in this case. We have been looking for all orders of castor beans in the past two years delivered to the US. Less than a grain of salt of ricin made airborne is lethal."

Fox News was next, "What makes you think that the Chicago Company did not know they were producing ricing infused incense sticks. That seems impossible that they didn't either take part in the attack or were just plain stupid?"

Matt stepped to the podium and responded, "I can't give you that information now as we are still investigating, but I will answer that question in time."

ABC News asked, "Should Catholics just stay away from church this Sunday in case the police missed their church?"

Stan took this question, "Besides the police visiting every Catholic church in America, we have notified all priests through their Bishops to use their own incense or use no incense in place of the sticks in case the local police missed a church,"

Questions continued for the next twenty minutes, pretty much on the same topics. Everyone answered what they could, and then the President closed with, "Again rest assured – we will not stop until whoever attacked America is identified. This will not take as long as it did to find bin Laden as we have a pretty good concrete lead. God Bless Everyone, and God Bless America. Thank you, and Denise will keep you updated daily on our progress."

With that, everyone left the Briefing Room and gathered in the Oval Office, and debriefed with Denise. She believed that all went exceptionally well. Stan thought so as well. Now the hard work of tracking down whoever had to take center stage. The President asked Stan to work closely with the FBI personally and to keep her informed daily. The team all left the Oval Office exhausted.

When Stan got back to his hotel room, he just sat down and thought through everything that had transpired in such a short span. Like Paris and San Bernardino, this attack had gotten through every bit of monitoring we do on a Worldwide basis minute by minute. And this attack was right in the CDC manual as a potential threat. His agency and his responsibility.

Growing up in a family where Stan's uncle was an alcoholic, he remembered the serenity prayer that was posted on his bedroom wall, "God, grant me the serenity to accept the things I cannot change, the courage to change the things I can, and the wisdom to know the difference." Stan had put a copy in his wallet on the day of Uncle Franklin's funeral. He had more often failed at "knowing the difference." How in the hell does a person figure that out? He couldn't change that Carol was President. He was happy for her but . . . serenity, not so much. What could they have changed? Nothing. What could they have done to have stopped this attack? Nothing. *"Cannot change" sucks.*

So, he thought, as the Director of the CDC, what could they have changed? What could they have done, if anything, to have stopped this attack? Stan knew that the answer was that the attack was in the "cannot change" column, but it was still bothering him, and he couldn't get this out of my mind. He just hated the sight of families dying in Freedom and the frustration of the medical staff there just making them comfortable instead of saving them.

The Catholic Supply Company closed its doors in Chicago with signs posted stating, "We are closed until further notice." Betty Wilcox had been swamped with calls from the press, and CNN was setting a satellite truck up in their parking lot, so she told everyone to go home with pay for now, and she closed down the operation. She asked her workers not to speak to the press and give them her number if they were contacted.

In Rome, Pope Alexander, through Cardinal Lenza, made a press release that read:

"I am deeply troubled by the tragic loss of life in Freedom, Montana. We are dealing with people that have no appreciation for the gift of life. They hate for the sake of hating. Their beliefs are flawed. World Peace Day, for all Catholics, was established so that 1.2 billion parishioners could together pray for peace in our lifetime. I urge every Catholic to attend Church on September 24th as you would do on Christmas or Easter Sunday. Be vigilant in your prayers that peace is essential for all cultures to thrive. Also, pray for the Catholic souls that perished in Freedom, Montana."

Cardinal Lenza had *not* shut his eyes since news of the Montana ricin attack broke. Perhaps the Pope would be so engrossed in salvaging his Papacy that he would not remember who recommended the green incense in the first place . . .

Stan called his father, who he knew had watched the press conference. "So, dad, have you any thoughts about how these incense sticks were produced, allowing the ricin to be airborne?"

"I have been thinking a lot about this, Stan. If someone had gotten into the factory that produced the incense sticks and at the right time dumped in ricin in a specific form, they would have had to know the composition of the incense and then added the ricin at the last stage.!!"

"Funny you have said that as there just might have been a person of interest that gained access at that time. We are still investigating but are on the trail for sure. Thanks, dad – I just wanted to talk and hear a friendly voice!"

Chapter 24 – Aleppo, Syria / Berkeley, California

While Stan Pace closed his eyes in Washington, Darcy Oban's inner manifesto of see-me-terrorist was starting to curl its edges. "Aazim, listen to those talking heads. FBI thinks it has a lead in Chicago. Shit, already? I thought Professor Pace was just up-bragging his son—shit. Maybe Nancy probably broke like the cheap glass she is—probably. Should have dumped her in one of those vats. But it worked. The ricin worked. Bootstrap CDC Director Stan Pace will lose a leg or two when he finally figures out that he was the dumb ass who OK'd the purchase of the ricin through his own father. Sweet. Damn timing stinks like a sewer. How could I know that some schmuck priest was going to do his damn peace day early? Bet they have been to my parents already, then on to Steven. That won't take long. Shit, Steven is just one big stinkweed need of pulling. When can I get out of here?"

"My father said patience, remember? XTREM will hide us both. It will take credit for the ricin attack in Montana and imply more ricin-tainted products in place—used by other churches and governments. XTREM wants to unravel all governance and faith-based organizations, get it?"

Aazim's tone was condescending and directive, both of which raised the tiny hairs on the back of Darcy's neck. She could not afford another mistake. Her left hand crawled back to quiet those hairs, but . . . *Who does this fool think he is? Another asshole trying to control me. Her ears were suddenly washed with wave gurgles, just lapping the shore. Her nostrils pushed into choking sand. Held arms numb. Shut up. We'll tell, you slut. You'll like it . . . everybody says so . . .*

"Darcy, we are headed to Al Bukamal, a Syrian town of about 250,000 on the Euphrates River near the Iraqi border. XTREM is pleased—you'll see."

"Yeah, right."

Berkeley, California

Seven thousand one hundred forty-eight miles away from Al Bukamal, in Berkeley, California, Steven Habid had watched both the initial CNN press conference in Freedom and the major press conference from the White House. Now he was panicked, especially since Darcy's cell phone was disconnected, and he had no way of talking to her or knowing where she was or what he should be doing.

He decided to call Darcy's mom and ask her why Darcy wasn't answering her phone. Amber answered and told him that she had gone to Syria to visit her grandparents and added, "Steven, this is crazy – the FBI was here asking about Darcy and any information she might have regarding a factory in Chicago. They have somehow tied it to the terrible deaths in Freedom, Montana."

Steven could not respond right away as all his breath had left his lungs. Finally, he gasped and said, "What do you mean, Mrs. Oban?"

"Well, evidently, the deaths in Freedom were caused by ricin in some incense used during Masses. The incense was processed at the Catholic Supplier here in Chicago," she explained.

Steven was frozen and said, "Well – if you hear from Darcy, tell her Steven called and wishes her good luck." He then hung up, not waiting for Mrs. Oban even to say a goodbye. His legs were weak, and his stomach was churning. He was almost positive that the FBI would eventually get to him, but he never was in Chicago at the supplier, and there was no trace of anything at his apartment, UCB labs, or his car.

He thought about taking off, but that would look suspicious. "Best just to keep doing what I would normally do," he thought. Freedom really screwed up the master plan and maybe him as well.

He reminded himself again that it wouldn't take long for the FBI to get to him if their "solid lead" had anything to do with Darcy. And after talking to her mother, it might be true. He knew that she hadn't reported to the classes at UCB that she had registered for, and that had alarmed him. He should have known better than to trust her. "She ran out on me," he said out loud. That had to be her plan through the entire ordeal. He felt just stupid not to have seen this coming. He repeatedly thought, "Darcy – how could you have done this to me?"

He was now worried and was thinking about what his parents would say if he were arrested. Shuttering and barely eating, he decided to continue working in the UCB lab like nothing was wrong and continued to prepare for his master's project presentation. He didn't know what else to do now that Darcy was out of the country, and the FBI's big lead just might steer them right to him. He again said out loud, "Keep my routine and just be the nerdy science guy that everyone hardly ever notices. Work alone on the master's project with ricing for Professor Pace." But again, he wanted to do this, and he wanted to go down in history as an important person.

Chapter 25 – FBI Offices – Chicago / Washington, D.C.

Agent Oltrogge and Blau were waiting anxiously for the Chicago Cyber Division to come up with anything from the Oban's cell phones and the parent's computers that might help them firmly connect Darcy and whomever else was responsible for this ricin attack. The head of the cyber lab came into Jerry's office with a list of potential names and numbers to consider.

"There is nothing on the parent's computers with any ties to ricin, castor beans, Freedom, Catholics, or XTREM," reported the cyber tech, "That's the bad news, but we did find one call on Darcy's cell phone to her grandparents in Syria as well as many back and forth to a Steven Habid. He has two addresses. One in Berkeley and another in Los Angles. He is a biochemical graduate student at UCB and Darcy Oban's lab partner. There is nothing else that looks suspicious." Jerry thanked the technician and went over to Agent Blau's office with the results.

"Sandy," Jerry asked, "Call Mrs. Oban on their landline and ask her if she has ever heard the name Steven Habid." Sandy made the call and was not surprised when Mrs. Oban said, "Our attorney has informed us not to answer any questions. Please refer any questions to the law firm of Young and Statton and ask for Mike Statton," and she hung up.

"Well, that went well," Sandy reported to Jerry. "She referred me to their attorney and hung up. She might be surprised if we arrest her as a terrorist, and no calls to her attorney will take place!"

"Relax, Sandy. Let's call Tim in D.C. and give him what we have and let him contact the L.A. office and go from there," Jerry said.

The call to Tim McLaughlin in Washington went just as Jerry thought. He would keep us posted and would contact the L.A. office at once. He also asked that we put a car outside the Oban's home 24/7 until the parents are officially cleared of any knowledge or any part of the ricin attack.

Tim called Stan and reported what he had, "Stan – I think it best that you fly out now to Berkeley and meet the L.A. agents as they pick up this Steven Habid. We just also linked him to a call he made a call to Syria from his cell phone, and the listening station in Virginia logged it in as follows – I'll read it to you, 'Another World Peace conversation – Berkeley, California to Aleppo, Syria. Initiated by cell phone number 312-555-1682 / owner Steven Habid. Time of call 22:16 EST - 90 seconds – nothing unusual.' Your knowledge of everything to do with ricin and what we know so far will help the agents in the interrogation. We will be enacting the Patriot Act, so Steven can scream lawyer all he wants, but since we don't know if there is any other imminent danger or other plans to attack America, he has no rights. You okay with this?"

Stan said he would be on the Gulfstream in thirty minutes and would bring Dr. Tom Matson, FBI Lab Director, with me. "Let them know that we will be there in 6 hours," he estimated.

"Thanks, Stan," answered Tim.

Stan quickly called his father and asked one question, "Do you know Steven Habid?" His father said that he was one of the two that secured permission to do the ricin project here on campus and that he and his lab partner were getting ready to present his master's project to the department and Stan himself. Stan told his father not to talk to anyone about this until he told him to.

He readied his office materials and a copy of the Patriot Act to read on the flight. While he knew that the L.A. FBI agents would know the law perfectly and would know what we could and could not do, he wanted to know just how far we could push Steven Habid. His concern that there may be another biochemical attack still was paramount. He, and maybe Darcy Oban, had pulled off a well-thought-out terrorist attack on our country. Was there more on the horizon? Stan shuttered at that thought and took off for the plane. The possibility that Steven used UCB's lab was also on his mind, and that would cause his father great harm. The voice reminded him, "control what you can, Stan."

Chapter 26 – Berkeley, CA / Rolling Hills, L.A.

Dr. Tom Matson and Stan landed at the Oakland International Airport and were greeted by FBI Agents Ken Jacobsen and Jeremy Lindaman. "Welcome to Oakland, Dr. Pace. I am Agent Jacobsen, and this is Agent Lindaman," Agent Jacobsen extended his hand. Stan introduced Tom to the agents, and they walked to the waiting black SUV.

"How long a drive is it to UCB?" Stan asked.

Agent Lindaman responded, "It's about 15 miles and takes an easy 30 minutes."

"Where is Steven Habid now?" asked Tom.

"We have two agents watching him," Ken said while getting into the SUV. "He is in the UCB Chemistry Lab working at this very moment. We will arrest him there as I wanted Dr. Matson to be able to look the lab over for anything suspicious before our forensics and cyber teams move in. We also have a search warrant. We have a team outside Steven's home in Rolling Hills, Los Angles. Very upscale neighborhood – average annual income is pushing $400,000. The father's name is Abeel, and the mother is Aryisha. Mom does not work, and the dad is an executive for a major clothing manufacturer. So we will wait until we arrest Steven to move in on the household with a warrant."

"Sounds good. I want to call my father, who is the Director of the Lab, and let him know we are coming. I will not explain anything until we have Steven in custody," Stan responded.

Jeremy asked, "Do you suspect the parents of any involvement in the Freedom attack?"

"First things first," Stan announced. "We have to find out exactly what, if any, involvement Steven has with the Freedom attack. Based on the number of calls between him and Darcy, I think he had some involvement. After Freedom, no calls from Darcy and a few to her unanswered cell phone calls from Steven. So clearly, Freedom must be the common denominator. We will see shortly."

Stan called his father, "Dad – I don't have time to talk, but we will be there shortly to arrest Steven Habid for questioning in the Freedom Attack. I will need to visit with you after the arrest. So please don't do anything out of your routine until we get there."

Professor Pace gasped and started to speak, and Stan cut him off and reiterated, "Not now, dad!"

As they approached the UCB Campus, the team all were impressed with how well-manicured everything was. The buildings were old but very well kept. They came in on Piedmont Avenue, then turned West on South Drive, and on our right was Gilman Hall, home of the Department of Chemical & Biomolecular Engineering. They noticed that Gilman Hall was built in 1917 and now on the historical register as they entered the building on the right. Stan couldn't help thinking what else it might be known for if Steven, in fact, was complicit in the Freedom attack.

Soon the over-buffed SUV turned onto a landscape-perfect Piedmont Avenue, then West on South Drive to the vintage 1917 Gilman Hall, home of the Department of Chemical & Biomolecular Engineering. No security. Typical and most unfortunate. Without attracting too much attention and bypassing the two plain-clothed FBI agents on their way down an original terrazzo-tiled floor, two agents and two directors located Lab 3, the common workspace of Steven Habid and the now-gone Darcy Oban.

"Are you Steven Habid?"

He was dressed in a typical white lab coat, wore glasses, and as he turned around, he said, "Yes, I am Steven Habid. How can I help you?" Steven was trying with all his might to stay calm and not to show any emotion except what an average person might show when the FBI asks that question. He knew nothing in the lab could tie him to the ricin attack, and he was very confident that there was nothing in his apartment either. Steven had cleaned it very well. He was shaking inside.

"Mr. Habid, you're under arrest for complicity in the Freedom, Montana ricin attack as well as the failed plan to implement ricin attack during masses in all American Catholic Churches," Agent Lindaman spoke distinctly and slowly as he approached Steven with handcuffs.

Habid's chem-lab glasses made a slight plastic-on-tile sound as they hit the floor, a useless noise against the backdrop of the slow-motion arrest. Steven fix-frozen on the handcuffs. *They have nothing. Only thing ricin in this lab I have permission for—nothing funnier than a clueless, dumb ass Pace standing there-- doesn't even realize he gave the OK—puzzled white-guy face. His dad had that same look, too. Apartment whistle clean. No witnesses—except Darcy. She rat me out? The crap I did for her. Nobody left but her . . .*

"This is insane – you are kidding," Steven shouted as he slipped off his lab coat and pounded his fists on the lab table. "I have rights, and I want a lawyer." He had heard this in every movie involving people being arrested.

Agent Lindaman continued as he confiscated Steven's cell phone, "We also have a warrant to search your car and apartment. Agent Jacobson, please escort Mr. Habid." The four men were deliberately keeping it low-key. Suits and white-jackets frequently cluttered the hallways of Gilman—federal grants were plentiful and monitoring abundant. The agents, and especially Stan, for his father's sake, wanted today to look no different.

Agent Lindaman added, "Have you ever heard of the Patriot Act? You have no rights for now and will be coming with us. We will also be serving warrants at your parents' home. I'm sure they will be pleased! Let's go."

Steven went silent, and he could picture his mother and father coming to their front door and being served warrants and potentially being taken in for questioning. He hated that, but they would live through it in time. As they were putting him in an SUV, he was joined by another agent in the back seat. Remaining silent was his goal as they would find nothing linking him to the ricin attack. The agent driving told the rest of the men there to meet at the FBI offices, and they pulled away.

"We will need to alert the University and whoever oversees Gilman Hall as we will need to close it down until the cyber and forensic teams have a chance to go through it," Tom explained. He then gave orders to each of the agents that were sitting on Steven to get to the administration building and make appropriate notifications. "Also, make sure that your FBI communications expert in LA is brought up to speed and is here because as soon as the yellow tape goes up, there will be tons of press here. Hell – they are probably already on their way after walking Habid out in cuffs. Cell phones are faster than any news agency!"

"I will gladly stay here with you, Tom, as the teams go through the building," Stan offered, but he was anxious to get to Steven to be part of the questioning that would go on for quite some time.

"No, Stan, I have this under control," Tom replied. "We have a lot to go through with this building, his car, and his apartment. Ken said they have his apartment roped off, and his car has been taken to the lab. So go ahead and go to the headquarters. I will catch up with you later."

"Thanks, Tom. I was hoping you would say that!" Stan chuckled, and he smiled back. Then, before he got into the SUV, he said to his father, who was standing at the entrance in shock, "Dad – don't worry – you did nothing to worry about. I will bring you up-to-date as soon as I know anything," and Stan got into the SUV, and the agent drove him back to the L.A. FBI Headquarters.

At the same time, Steven Habid was being loaded into the SUV; two FBI agents walked up to the massive front door of the home of Abeel and Aryisha Habid. Mr. Habid answered the door, and the agents showed them their credentials and read to him a warrant to search the house and take all computers, cell phones, iPads, and other electronic communication devices. His wife came to the entryway and listened.

" What is this about," Abeel boldly asked.

"We have reason to believe that your son Steven may have been part of the planned ricin attack on all Catholic Churches in the United States. This attack killed 153 men, women, and children in Freedom, Montana. He has been arrested as a terrorist under the Patriot Act," the agent explained. "We would like you and your wife to come with us down to the FBI LA field office, 11000 Wilshire Boulevard Suite 1700, while the cyber and forensic teams go through your home."

Abeel had just about lost it halfway through the agent's explanation, replying, "This is just crazy. Steven is a nerd that loves science and would never be involved with anything like you are suggesting. Aryisha, let's go and straighten out this mess. The news agencies will love the story of the FBI again, targeting Muslims. Can I call my attorney on the way?"

"I'm sorry, Mr. Habid," the agent answered. "I have to take that cell phone from you as part of the warrant. You are welcome to use mine."

They all walked out to the SUV to drove down to the FBI offices. Other agents were wearing jackets with white letters on them, as you see on the CSI television shows, were entering the house. Abeel looked back as they pulled away and had a terrible feeling go through his system. He thought about all the time Steven spent in the lab and that he hardly ever came home anymore, except when he had to. Quickly he erased those thoughts as there was no way Steven could have done such a thing. He could picture himself with Steven and Aryisha being interviewed on the *Today Show* for being arrested and detained by the FBI for suspicions that were not founded.

Chapter 27 - L.A. FBI Field Office

Stan was informed that Steven's parents were on their way with agents to the Field Office and that Steven was situated in an interview room ready for interrogations to begin. Agent Jeremy Lindaman was well trained in interrogation and would start the interview with Steven. He asked Stan to sit in but not to talk unless he asked him to.

Stan asked, "I have minimal experience with this process but could get into the production of ricin if Steven starts talking." *How could this have happened in Dad's lab without his knowing? What did happen? Christ, Carol . . .* Stan's face was rock outside and slush inside.

Jeremy smiled and said, "I went to a training session, and a police officer from Riley County said, 'We (officers) are like used car salesmen. But instead of selling a junky car to someone, we have to sell the idea that confessing is the best thing to do'. So our goal with Steven is to obtain a confession and find out if there are other attacks planned, what his involvement was with Darcy Oban, and who else was involved in this planned attack. The sessions will all be recorded both video and audio."

"Ok, Jeremy," Stan responded. "You have the lead, and I will listen unless you ask me to join in." Clearly, he was a pro at this.

We went into the small interrogation room. There were three chairs and a table at which Steven was sitting behind. He was cuffed to an iron circle on the table. He looked up as we entered and said, "You can't make me talk about something I do not know of. This entire thing is a mistake, as you will soon find out."

For someone that was not going to say anything, Steven already had broken that statement, thought Jeremy, who then said, "My name is Agent Jeremy Lindaman, and this is Dr. Stan Pace, Director of the Center for Disease Control. First off, I want to let you know about the Patriot Act under which you have been arrested. I will just read a portion to you, and if you have any questions, I will gladly answer them."

"Section 802 of the USA PATRIOT Act (Pub. L. No. 107-52) expanded the definition of terrorism to cover "domestic," as opposed to international terrorism. A person engages in domestic terrorism if they do an act "dangerous to human life" that is a violation of the criminal laws of a state or the United States if the act appears to be intended to: (i) intimidate or coerce a civilian population; (ii) influence the policy of a government by intimidation or coercion; or (iii) to affect the conduct of a government by mass destruction, assassination or kidnapping. Additionally, the acts have to occur primarily within the territorial jurisdiction of the United States and if they do not, may be regarded as international terrorism."

"Any questions so far, Steven," asked Jeremy.

"No, sir," replied Steven.

Steven maintained his silent tabletop stare.

Lindaman continued, "We have evidence that you and Berkeley lab partner, Darcy Oban, made ricin and orchestrated its infusion into incense sticks delivered by a Chicago manufacturer to every American Catholic Church. This plan failed a nationwide attack but caused the deaths of 153 men, women, and children in Freedom qualifies as terrorism under the Patriot Act. As a result, you have no rights. Let me repeat, Mr. Oban, you have no rights."

Steven did not look up or respond. *They're trying to trick me. Get me to cough up, Darcy. Has she already coughed me up? They don't have anything but smoke—not even a mirror. Don't blink.*

Jeremy continued, "We have evidence that you and Darcy Oban made ricin, infused it in the incense sticks that when burned would make the ricin airborne, and had it delivered to every Catholic Church in the USA. It doesn't make any difference to us as to what your role was, but any involvement means you are complicit." Jeremy knew that their evidence on Steven was currently only phone calls to Darcy, but Steven didn't know this.

"That's a lot of information in a short time, Steven. Again, do you have any questions?" asked Jeremy.

Stan was watching this exchange and noticed that Steven's head had dropped a little bit, and he was staring at the middle of the table instead of at Jeremy. So if nothing else, he may have known what Darcy was doing, and he would also be prosecuted for, but maybe not for life.

Steven said, "No questions. Can I have something to drink, please?"

"In a while," responded Jeremy.

"So Steven, I think Darcy had this plan and asked you to help." Jeremy supposed. "Since you and she were close friends or lovers, you agreed...."

Steven looked up for the first time. Agent Lindaman had found his trigger. "We were just friends . . . just friends. Masters project together. You know, with Professor Pace. He got CDC's permission for us to purchase just a small about of castor beans for the project."

"Record notation: strike the last two sentences." Lindaman pressed on to set the hook. "So as a close friend, Oban needed your help with this plan—she couldn't swing it alone. Against your better judgment, you agreed—as Oban's friend. She might have held things over you like Muslim-me superiority or poor-victim-me, doubting your decision-making? If you would have said 'no,' she would have refused to see you and/or pulled out as your master's partner? Oban was good at making you afraid, right?"

Steven had fallen back to silence. Stan Pace watched his slender fingers curl, uncurl, and curl again.

No response from Steven. Jeremy continued, "You are a brilliant young man Steven. UCB professors say you are one of their brightest biochemistry graduate students. Professor Pace indicated that you were outstanding as a student." Jeremy was just guessing but was probably correct. "So, Darcy was the mastermind according to our information, and you just went along with what she requested?"

No response from Steven, but his posture switched to a more jittery stance.

"Mr. Habid," Lindaman's voice escalated slowly with purpose, "your case will benefit by giving us information about the plan. So you won't leave here, got it?" A sudden buzzer sound sent the frustrated agent from the room.

"Sorry for the interruption," said the face-weary forensic tech. "Initial results from the USC science lab (except for the locked vault containing the ricin for Habid's Master's project), his apartment, and car are all ricin-negative. But . . . look at this." The tech cautiously pulled a photo from a large tan envelope and held it up like a 3-year-old hoping for parental approval on the latest coloring project.

Agent Lindaman looked at the photo. Then looked at the tech. Then held it closer to be sure what he saw was true. "Perfect." As the tech walked two feet taller down the hallway, Lindaman re-opened the door to the interrogation room and motioned Stan Pace out.

"What have you got?" Stan's worry about his father and the cement-faced kid in the next room had stretched his patience and focus

Lindaman put the photo in the Director's hand. Stan stepped two tiles out into the hall, turning the evidence upward to the twitching fluorescent light. "God. Get agents to my dad's house fast . . . he isn't in his office and doesn't answer his phone. He was this kid's teacher." Stan clutched the photo as it if were another spit wad for that Rhoda-girl long ago in row 12 . . . soggy-chewed and waiting for the hurl.

"On it. Get what you can in there—the tape is rolling." Lindaman nodded Pace back into the interrogation room and disappeared.

Steven Habid was as the Agent and Director had left him, chained to the table but bent-shriveled in his fight-or-flight machinations. Stan placed the photo face-down on the table in front of him as he positioned himself directly across from the young scientist. *Don't let this kid see fear. No sweating. This is not the Middle East. Does he know where my dad is? Shit, I can't let Carol down. Want a drink so damn bad. Why can't I remember this punk and his punk friend with the ricin experiment?* "Mr. Habid, I am Dr. Stan Pace, CDC Director. Your Professor's son, as Agent Lindaman indicated earlier. Forensics teams have been all over the UCB lab, your car, and your apartment. No ricin." Stan noted the ever-faint up-curl of Steven Habid's lips. *Jesus, he did it. How could this young dumb-ass do it? Not him, her.*

"I am sure you are aware, forensic teams take photos of every square inch." Stan placed his hands on the up-side-down photo before him. *Don't shake. Hold fingers still.* Like this photo, for instance, from your apartment." Stan turned the image over and slowly pushed it forward. Habid forgot himself and leaned in for the look. Stan watched closely to see how his detainee would react to the picture of *one* castor bean lying on what appeared to be the floor under his apartment stove.

Nothing. Habid's face and voice had died, cold-dead and buried. Steven looked away from the photo to the wall behind Stan's head.

I want to beat the shit out of you, shithead. So easy. You'd talk. Stop it. This is not Iraq. Cameras here. "You know, this is a brilliant plan . . . incense sticks for Catholic mass infused with ricin. It might be possible to have a future by helping the FBI—they do it all the time—hire professionals to stop other professionals. Not too late. We know you didn't start this. You have been duped by someone else. You are falling alone, correct? Why would you want to protect that? Is she worth your life?"

Still, Steven Habid was silent. *She did leave me. She is not worth my life. Love her. Throw Darcy under the bus? I could say she used my apartment when I was not there; that must have been how the castor bean got under the stove. I could say that Darcy just wanted to order more castor beans—I had no idea why. She always does what she wants. She was in my apartment many times when I wasn't there. Don't speak. Just think.*

"Perfect," Jeremy responded. He opened the door to the interrogation room and asked Stan to come out.

"Stan – we found only the castor bean under the stove in Steven's apartment," Jeremy explained. "Nothing in the science lab except for his approved master's project or anything else yet from his car. They have brought back bags of potential evidence from the apartment, but that will take some time."

"I agree, Stan," Jeremy said as we entered the room. Jeremy had brought a bottle of water in for Steven, who thanked him.

"So, tell me, Steven, why did the forensics team find one castor bean under your stove against the back wall?"

Steven was thinking quickly, and while he cleaned his apartment perfectly well, including bleaching some areas, he never looked under the stove. Shit – how could one bean have gotten that far away from the table they worked on. He responded, "I have no clue, Dr. Pace. I have only had this apartment for a little over a year. Someone else may have used castor beans for something, but I have no clue." He squirmed a little as he took a drink from the water bottle.

Stan continued, "So that is interesting. Castor bean seeds are easily purchased, but the actual castor bean is much harder to come by. So again, Steven, tell me about castor beans and making ricin. As a scientist, you know it is fairly easy. This was part of your master's project, which was approved."

"As a scientist, I do know how to make ricin, but I have never purchased castor beans or made ricin except in the confines of our project," Steven barked. He liked that the CDC Director referred to him as a scientist. He smiled.

Stan noticed that Steven had smiled after he had referred to him as a scientist, so he continued, "You know, the person or persons responsible for this plan and attack will no doubt go down in history and will help rewrite CDC protocol for dealing with biochemical threats to our nation. If you were part of this plan, you could help us determine what needs to be changed, never allowing this to happen again. The FBI hires arrested hackers all the time to work with them to foil cyber-attacks. Our agency was amazed that incense sticks were used to make ricin airborne. That is the deadliest form of ricin. Brilliant plan."

Stan was careful not to promise Steven anything, which he did not. Instead, he wanted him to see that he was sincere and might help him. Clearly, the plan was brilliant and never used before—kind of like using passenger planes as weapons as in 9/11.

Steven was quiet, looking up to the ceiling, thinking, or dreaming. He then said, "What if I knew someone that could give you information regarding the plan and attack, but that person was no longer around, so you wouldn't be able to visit with them?"

Jeremy jumped in, saying, "That would be a great first step, Steven. If, in fact, this person was the mastermind and you only knew of the plan and did not participate in the planning, then you might get off with a lesser sentence, or maybe just probation." Jeremy knew it was ok to lie to a person being interrogated. It was a perfectly legal tool. He used words like "might," making sure that no solid promises were on the table.

Steven was thinking. How could he throw Darcy under the bus without implicating himself? He could say that she used his apartment when he was not there, and that must have been how the castor bean got under the stove. He could say that ordering the larger portion of the beans besides those needed for their master's project was the only part he had in the plan. That just might fly, he thought!

Chapter 28 - LA FBI Field Office

The interrogation was in progress, and the cyber team had determined that Steven's parents never made any suspicious calls to anyone, including Darcy's cell phone. All their laptops and computers were clean of any references to ricin except as a news blurb, and nothing was found of any substance in their home by the forensics team. A technician tapped the door to the interrogation room and gave Jeremy this written information.

Jeremy said, "Stan – let's take a break and let Steven think seriously about what he wants to share with us. Oh, by the way, Steven. You also need to explain your 90-second cell phone call to someone in Syria talking about the Pope's Peace Day."

Steven gulped as he remembered that Darcy's phone battery was low, and she asked if she could use his. How was he going to explain that, he thought to himself? This was getting out of hand, and it looked like he was the mastermind and not Darcy. Had she done everything like the cell phone to set him up?

We went out into the hall, and Dr. Tom Matson was back from UCB and wanted to sit down and review everything we had to that point from UCB and Chicago and said, "Before you both go back at Steven, let's see where we are on all fronts. This might help you leverage Steven."

Tom continued, "In Chicago, we know that ricin was infused into the liquid incense with a bonding material that hardened into sticks that were sent out to every Catholic Church in the nation. Darcy was undoubtedly responsible for the infusion when she came to the company alone before production started on Monday. She probably killed the homeless man in the parking lot when she exited the company. We found traces of ricin on the equipment at the plant. We also know that her parents had no clue what she was up to, and she went to Aleppo, Syria, before the Freedom attack to visit her grandparents. She did not return."

"Furthermore," Tom was referring to his notes, "We know that it appears that Steven's parents also had no clue as to anything he was doing helping Darcy in making ricin out of castor beans. We are chasing a lead on where the castor beans were ordered from and where they were delivered. Steven's lab and his car are of no help. His apartment contained one castor bean under the stove. They probably worked at his apartment, crushing the beans and extracting the ricin from the mush.

Darcy took the ricin with her in a rental car back to Glencoe, Illinois, where she gained the trust of her high school friend working at the Chicago company that won the bid for the incense sticks to gain access using a key she fabricated using her camera. The rest is history. Freedom went a week early, and while 153 people perished, up to 79 million were spared."

Stan commented, "Jeremy, I think our next step with Steven is to tell him that we have arrested his parents for complicity in the ricin attack as they were paying for his apartment and that they must forfeit their house, cars, and belongings under the Patriot Act. He is too weak to be able to let that happen. I think he is ready to tell us more anyway. What do you think?"

Jeremy agreed, and they went back in to push a little harder on Steven. Jeremy first asked Steven to explain the cell phone call to Syria.

"I don't' remember making any calls to Syria ever!" Steven was firm.

"So, you are saying someone else used your phone to make this call, and you were not aware of this?" Jeremy pushed.

"Yes – that is what I am saying. I don't know anyone in Syria."

Jeremy then asked Stan to start as he had established some trust with Steven before the break. He started, "Steven, I have some troubling news for you. We have arrested your parents for complicity in the Freedom attack and the master plan to kill millions of Catholics. Under the Patriot Act, they will also forfeit all their possessions. We have enough evidence that puts them in the same situation you are, knowing about the plan and not doing anything to stop it. Therefore, we will not be visiting with you further as we will place you in confinement. You are not allowed an attorney until we can confirm that there are no more biochemical threats planned to your knowledge in the USA. Do you understand what I have just explained to you?"

Steven put his hands to his face and started crying. Everything that Stan had ever heard about interrogation meant that Steven had given up and would soon tell the truth, but not to push him until he did. Jeremy and Stan waited ten minutes, and then Steven started.

"You have to understand," Steven was crying and almost choking as he spoke, "My parents did not know any part of this plan. It was all Darcy and me from the start. We had talked a lot as we worked together for countless hours in the lab about how our lives, especially since 9/11, had changed. From always being bullied because we looked like Middle Eastern people and the fact that we were Muslims."

"Every time I got on an airplane, people would stare at me and point at me as they were talking to their seatmates. Likewise, no one would even date Darcy because she looked the same. Our hatred towards America and her hatred of the Catholic Church grew and grew throughout our growing-up years."

He stopped for a moment and wiped his eyes with his shirt sleeve, "The XTREM movement gave us hope that America would start taking Muslims more seriously and not hate us because of our beliefs. Darcy called an XTREM friend of hers in Syria and made them aware of the plan using my cell phone. I'm sure they will take credit for the Freedom attack and be sorry that up to 79 million had not died as they should have. Will you please release my parents; I have told you everything. Oh – and there are no other biochemical plans that we had anything to do with as far as I know."

Stan asked Steven where he got the castor beans and where they were delivered. He shared this information, and Jeremy said, "As soon as we verify your story, we will let your parents go."

"Can I see them?" Steven begged.

"I can arrange that," Jeremy replied, "but just for a short time.

Stan and Jeremy left the room and went to the conference room where Tom had been watching the interview, "WOW – you were right. The parents were the key. I'm glad we reviewed everything. This sure puts everything in perspective. Now the fun begins. We should get back to Washington, D.C., and review everything with the NSC, and then the President will no doubt want to make a speech to the nation. I might add the country is still very nervous as you might imagine."

"I agree, Tom," Stan stated, "we need to get back sooner than later. Can we keep a lid on this until we get back tonight and then meet with President Sutton?"

"For sure, Stan," Tom sighed. "The press knows that something is up, but nothing specific. We won't release the parents until the morning after they see Steven. That should give us enough lead time to accomplish everything we need to do. There are always leaks, so we need to work quickly."

We thanked the LA FBI agents for doing a terrific job and asked them to keep us posted. They were still going through everything with a fine-tooth comb. Finally, they took us to the airport in one of their black SUVs, and we boarded the Gulfstream for the flight back to Washington, D.C. Stan called the President's Chief of Staff and briefed him on the findings. He said he would schedule an emergency meeting of the NSC for 9:00 a.m. EST.

As Stan drifted off to sleep, he wondered just how much *Rewards for Justice* would place on Darcy Oban's head. Abu Bakr al-Baghdadi, the current XTREM leader, had a ten-million-dollar reward on his head. The NSC meeting in the morning would be most interesting.

As he was thinking about everything on the jet, Steven was brought to another and larger conference room by Jerry and another agent. His parents were waiting to see him. They had already been briefed by Jeremy and been told that they had to stay across the table from Steven. Only after the meeting was over could they make any physical contact.

Steven was so glad to see his parents and started crying again. He said, "I am so sorry, mom and dad. I didn't think about how much trouble this possibly would cause for you. I love you with all my heart, but I also am not sorry for what I did. I know that I am a disappointment to you, and we will probably never be together as a family again." He lowered his head and stared at his handcuffs.

Steven's mother was crying right, along with Steven. His father was stoic. He finally said, "We are disappointed, for sure, Steven. Your life as you know it has just changed forever. Our lives have also just changed forever. You have brought shame to our home and heritage. While I cannot forgive you, you know I still love you." Steven just stared through his tears at both of his parents.

With that, Abeel helped his wife up, who was still crying, and said, "There is nothing more to discuss at this point. We are leaving." Aryisha hugged her son for a long time, weeping on his shoulder. Then, they left the room with Steven sitting back down at the table with his head down. He did not look back up at his parents as they left the room.

Abeel knew that he and his wife would be treated as pariahs, and the press would be parked outside their home as soon as the FBI announced Steven's arrest. He remembered seeing movies and actual news footages of press members blocking driveways and workplaces trying to get interviews or glimpses of family members.

He called his attorney to seek some help and to give him the situation as he knew it. His attorney told him that he might also lose his job if this situation brought negative attention to his company. Again, the term "nexus" was used. His attorney said that legally meant that if what a person does in their private life affects their job, they can be dismissed for cause.

In this case, even though Abeel and his wife had nothing to do with the attack, the negative press using the family name might be enough for a company to look for separation. Abeel thanked him, and they scheduled a meeting the following day to look over everything. His world that he knew this morning would never be the same.

The University of California at Berkeley's in-house attorney held an emergency press conference stating, "Today, one of our graduate students, Steven Habid, was arrested by the FBI as a suspect in the ricin attack in Freedom, MT. No evidence of any involvement using the laboratories at UCB have been found and are not expected." The attorney took no questions and stepped away from the microphones.

They left out the part about Steven's and Darcey's approved Master's projects involving Ricin. That would surely come out later, and Professor Pace would be potentially in a tough spot.

Chapter 29 – Washington, D.C.

At promptly 9:00 a.m. EST, the National Security Council met at the White House. President Sutton had asked the Joint Chiefs also to attend the meeting. Everyone stood when the President entered the room, and she motioned everyone to be seated. Tom and Stan had dictated a summary of what they knew to date on the biochemical attack in Freedom, MT – the master plan that failed, and the arrest and confession of Steven Habid in L.A. Everyone had a chance to review the abbreviated report before the NSC meeting.

President Sutton began, "Well – we have come a long way in a short period of time. Thanks to the FBI and the CDC for all their hard work on this terrible tragedy. Needless to say, it is just a matter of time before XTREM takes full credit for the attack on America, and we want to get ahead of their announcement. Press Secretary Robinson and I will formulate a speech to the country to be given at 1:00 p.m. EST. Notify all the news agencies, and let's not take any questions, as the investigation is still ongoing."

"Madam President," Stan actually raised his hand – a habit from so many years in public schools, "We are 100% sure that Steven Habid and Darcy Oban had only one plan that only partially succeeded. We must encourage everyone in America to remember to follow the *See Something Say Something* program. There will be more attempts on our country. When we stop them, of course, we don't advertise. This plan was well designed and, unfortunately, brilliant. No one would have thought of this exact threat, just like we didn't catch 9/11. Our lenses must widen, and we need fresh eyes and ears looking at everything differently every day. I hope you can convey this in your address."

"Thank you, Dr. Pace," the president responded. "We will work some of your thoughts into the address. After the address, I also want to meet with just the Joint Chiefs, Matt Harvey, and you, Dr. Stan Pace. Again – well-done everyone and promptly." The president stood up, as did everyone in the room, and she walked out.

Before the press conference, President Cortney received a message from NATO, indicating that for the second time in history since NATO was formulated, the Allies invoked the principle of Article 5. The first time was less than 24 hours after 911. She reviewed Article 5;

Article 5

"The Parties agree that an armed attack against one or more of them in Europe or North America shall be considered an attack against them all, and consequently they agree that, if such an armed attack occurs, each of them, in exercise of the right of individual or collective self-defense recognized by Article 51 of the Charter of the United Nations, will assist the Party or Parties so attacked by taking forthwith, individually and in concert with the other Parties, such action as it deems necessary, including the use of armed force, to restore and maintain the security of the North Atlantic area.

Any such armed attack and all measures taken as a result thereof shall immediately be reported to the Security Council. Such measures shall be terminated when the Security Council has taken the measures necessary to restore and maintain international peace and security."

She set aside the message and copy of Article 5 and was thankful that NATO recognized how severe this attack on America was and could have been much worse.

President Sutton and Denise Robinson worked on an address and walked into the East Room in the White House at promptly 1:00 p.m. EST. Secretary Robinson said, "The President will address the nation and bring everyone up to speed on the Freedom, Mt. ricin attack, as well as the failed attack on all Catholic Churches in the United States. There will be no questions following the President's address due to the ongoing investigations. Ladies and gentleman of the press and America, the President of the United States."

President Sutton stepped up the podium and began, "Fellow Americans – I want to bring you up to speed on the investigation regarding the ricin attack in Freedom, MT, and the failed attack on all American Catholic Churches. The was a Domestic terrorist attack carried out by Steven Habid, Rolling Hills, LA, and Darcy Oban, Glencoe, ILL, both are biochemistry graduate majors at the University of California Berkeley. Mr. Habid is in custody under the Patriot Act in Los Angles and has confessed his role in the plan and outlined Ms. Oban's role. Ms. Oban is believed to be hiding somewhere in Syria, well protected by XTREM, who will soon certainly formally take responsibility for the ricin attack on American soil."

She continued, "I want to thank all the agencies that worked so quickly to get to the bottom of this attack and for NATO invoking Article 5. We have had our share of terrorist attacks, including 9/11 – Boston Marathon – San Bernardino, and now Freedom, Montana, to only mention a few. But, as always, America will be stronger than before, and we will prevail. There is no place in the world that Darcy Oban will be able to hide that we will not find her. The Justice Reward Program has just placed a fifteen-million-dollar reward for information leading to the location, arrest, or conviction of Darcy Oban," the President paused and glared at the camera.

"This attack, or one like it, could happen anywhere in the world. It is time for world powers to join efforts to stop XTREM and everything they stand for. Their ideology is flawed and cannot be tolerated. We were fortunate that up to 79 million USA Catholics, 25% of the 319 million Americans, did not perish in this well-planned ricin attack. We cannot wait any longer for any country to sustain a catastrophic loss like almost happened in America and then react. I will be contacting leaders from various countries to formulate a plan to rid our world of XTREM and everything they stand for."

"In conclusion – as Americans, your eyes and ears are what will thwart most threats. If you *See Something, Say Something*. Agencies will quickly investigate any information you share. We pray for the people in Freedom, Montana, who have lost so much. We will never forget you. God Bless You all, and God Bless the United States of America."

President Cortney turned and walked away from the press members in the East Room. What no one could see were the tears in her eyes, thinking about the losses in Freedom. She would soon visit there.

Within minutes, simultaneously, the press in Chicago and Los Angeles rushed to the Oban's and Habid's homes and set up equipment for the long haul. Both families, on the advice of their attorneys, had checked into hotels under assumed names.

What the press does best is to start digging into every aspect of Steven and Darcy's lives from birth to the present date. So teachers, professors, friends, neighbors, coaches, relatives, and employers would all be contacted in the next few days, asking probing questions on recorded video, trying to give the public a glimpse into the lives of Steven and Darcy and why they would do such a terrible thing.

Clearly the press would find ample evidence that they had been radicalized, starting at early ages. They experienced unchecked harassment and bullying. It all came together when they met at UCB and were part of a radical splinter group. To the world, they were sincere, brilliant college students that had tremendous potential as scientists. Unfortunately, they were invisible to authorities, and the word "stealth" was used in the press to describe both of them.

Darcy Oban's picture was published in every newspaper globally with a fifteen-million-dollar reward posted under her name. Steven's picture was posted next to hers with the caption "in custody" across his face.

Chapter 30 – Syria/ Vatican City

One hour after the President of the United States finished her address to the country and the world, XTREM High Commander Addar Ismail posted a video. The speech was brief but very worrisome to anyone in the world that was not part of this ideology.

"To the President of the United States and all other infidels in the World. In Freedom, Montana, the ricin attack was an XTREM, well-planned attack initially targeting up to 79 million Catholics. The stupid Catholics of Freedom, Montana, went against the wishes of their Pope and celebrated World Catholic Peace Day a week early. They now rest in peace with their God. This attack on American soil demonstrates that XTREM can and will someday be the divine rulers of the Earth. There will be many more attacks in many forms currently being planned everywhere in the world. We will not be stopped. The oceans once protecting countries are no longer insurmountable. We are everywhere and growing. A special note to President Sutton – America is weak and afraid. You, Madame President, as a woman, are weak and afraid. We will see you soon, Madam President. Allah Akbar!"

Al Bukamal, Syria

Darcy and Aazim watched the President's speech on CNN and the XTREM leader's video claiming responsibility for the ricin attack on Catholics in America. Darcy thought that fifteen million dollars was a lot of money to tempt someone to turn her in. However, Aazim explained that bin Ladan's reward was much higher, and no one turned him in. Still, she was concerned and knew that someday her fate was inevitable. But her name would go down in history for a cause she believed in with all her heart.

Vatican City

Following the President of the United States address and the XTREM response, Pope Alexander also made an address to the World, "It is with my deepest sympathy regarding the deaths of Catholics in Freedom, Montana that I am speaking today on behalf of the 1.2 billion Catholics worldwide. A tragedy of enormous proportions has been stopped, with XTREM attempting to silence up to 79 million American Catholics when they were praying for peace. The losses in Freedom were senseless. The Vatican will no longer remain silent regarding XTREM atrocities. We hope and pray for a peaceful ending to what now has risen to excessive levels of hatred. With that said, the world powers must unite to end XTREM ideologies."

Chapter 31 – Washington, D.C.

President Sutton, her Press Secretary and Director of National Intelligence had watched the video where XTREM was claiming responsibility and making threats to the USA and other countries in the world. So president Sutton said to Matt Harvey, "Let's go down and meet with the Joint Chiefs (JCS), Dr. Stan Pace, yourself, Matt."

Matt entered the situation room, and Stan could see that he was on a mission just by the way he rushed into the room. He announced The President would like to meet with the JCS, me, and you, Dr. Pace right now if that still works for everyone?" Everyone nodded affirmatively, and Matt left the room to get the President. Stan was fascinated that in a few minutes that he would be part of a meeting with the Chairman of the Joint Chiefs, the Vice Chairman of the Joint Chiefs, and Service Chiefs from the Air Force, Marine Corps, the Navy, the Army, and the National Guard.

Less than five minutes later, they were all seated around the table. Stan was also wondering how the President would react to the XTREM announcement and could see that she was very focused on something. So, she started, "Thank you all for making time in your schedule for an initial planning session on what our next steps should be both domestically as well as internationally. XTREM's threats take on an entirely different meaning after the ricin attack that almost was the worst single disaster the world has ever seen. So, let's get started."

Matt started, "We need to increase our monitoring of all communications and not take some things with a grain of salt like the call from Mr. Habid or Ms. Oban to a friend in Syria, which turned out to be an XTREM member. The log from the Clarksville, VA listening station noted another discussion regarding World Peace Day not needing follow-up. I think we need to follow up on all communications to Syria and all other Middle Eastern countries. Every call is now an important call to follow up, no matter how frivolous it seems."

He continued, "While Steven Habid and Darcy Oban were US citizens, both their parents were naturalized citizens from Syria. While what I am about to say will sound very intrusive, I think we need to covertly monitor communication traffic at higher levels for all naturalized citizens from the Middle East until the threat levels start to subside."

As everyone looked at Matt for what seemed to be minutes of silence, then he said, "Under *the Foreign Intelligence Surveillance Act (FISA)*, we can get a FISA warrant to do this monitoring per our legal department legally. Of course, this would require a lot of overtime as well as some additional help, but it can be done, and under the circumstances, I don't think we would have any trouble securing the warrant."

The President responded, "I concur, and let's get this done ASAP, Matt." He nodded back in response.

Stan followed Matt, "At the CDC, we remain concerned that a chemical attack, like the one in Freedom and planned for all Catholics at their Peace Day Masses, could be replicated in some fashion targeting other groups. While it may not come in the form of ricin, many other possibilities would be equally as deadly. In addition, we are concerned that this recent incident could potentially give other radicalized Americans some ideas that they had not considered previously. So, the CDC will be working more closely with all companies that sell anything that could potentially be used for a chemical attack."

"We also need to watch more closely the imports like castor beans delivered to a warehouse in L.A. from South America that the UCB biochemistry graduate students used to make ricin. The beans were ordered using a phony invoice from UCB and were not marked as castor beans. This was too easy and, in the future, cannot happen."

Stan continued and addressed his following comments to General Justin Else, Chairman of the Joint Chiefs, "I may be out of line, so please stop me General if you think I am, but as an Army Ranger, I have seen my share of military combat in both Iraq and Afghanistan. Unfortunately, the entire XTREM existence is based on an ideology, and until we can render this ideology silent, they will continue to thrive."

Continuing, "I recently read a passage from *The Babylon Code* by McGuire and Anderson that stayed with me on page 52:"

"XTREM is on a jihadist rampage now. Robbing. Killing. Destroying. Enslaving. Raping. Torturing. Beheading. Because XTREM is a satanic movement. This is not mere terrorism. This is genocide. These are demon-possessed people making blood sacrifices to their god, and if they are not stopped, they will murder millions and bring down one mid-eastern regime after another. As Americans, we dare not turn a blind eye to this threat. If we don't defeat the jihadists over there, they are coming here."

"So, I see this in two steps; one is the need to quickly go into Syria and Iraq with 20,000 special forces from ten countries. These countries will join us after watching what almost happened here. They don't need training and could be deployed in days, not months. Secondly, a coalition needs to keep a presence in both countries to help rebuild their infrastructures and help them see that what XTREM stood for is not something the world will tolerate."

President Sutton leaned back, thinking of previous issues presented to her regarding the XTREM fight. Airpower alone would not do the trick, and that Syria was a much different problem as it was just in total chaos. In her campaign for President, there were mixed feelings among her opponents regarding boots on the ground. The main fear was that we would again get into a long war. But a short mission using only Special Forces joined by nine other countries had her attention. She leaned over to hear General Else's response.

General Else responded, "Your ideas Dr. Pace have merit and have already been discussed by the Joint Chiefs. The President can authorize our special forces to work with other countries to attack XTREM, just as we do with drones and bombers working now with other countries in the region. The War Powers Act of 1973 does not allow a president to declare war. Still, as we are already working with other countries against XTREM without boots on the ground, a two-week special forces joint mission combined with all the resources already in place would not violate the Act. These resources include four warships in the Mediterranean Sea – USS Mahas, USS Ramage, USS Gavey, and the USS Barry – all guided-missile destroyers. The USS George H.W. Bush Aircraft Carrier was also positioned there as well. In addition, command (JOSC) operatives were ready for drone attacks as they too were already present."

The President sat forward in her chair and paused, then said, "General, what countries including NATO do you see helping us in this action?"

The General opened up his briefcase and passed out a document marked Top Secret, "Here is a list of the top special forces in the world, and the Joint Chiefs have already made inquiries with their counterparts who have all indicated that they now have a chip in the game. These forces are the best of the best. No plans were presented or discussed, but they are interested in further discussions at higher levels." He then reviewed the following list:

The Special Operation Forces

Jordanian Armed Forces

German Kommando Spezialkräfte

Turkish Maroon Berets

Russian Spetsnaz

French Naval Commandos

USA MARSOC (U. S. Marine Corps Forces Special Operations Command)

England's MI-6

Unit 777 in Egypt

U.S. Army Rangers

U.S. Army Green Berets

U.S. Delta Force

Israeli's Shayetet 13

U.S. Navy Seals

British SAS.

"Madame President," General continued, "again, these are the best of the best, and with your leadership in contacting the powers to be in each country, this coalition could be put into action actually within a week. This would have to remain a covert operation until the first attacks would take place. We also have an initial plan for the attack based on current XTREM occupations." The General then pulled out another Top-Secret Document and put it up on the screen. "Here is the initial simultaneous attack plan utilizing 20,000 special forces:"

1.Ayn-al-Arab South East to Raqqa

2.Aleppo South East to Raqqa

3.North-East of Damascus to Deirez Zaul to Qaim

4.Hasaka East to Mosul / Mosul South to Hawija

5. Ramada East to Baghdad then North to Samana

The General continued, "We also now have confirmed that XTREM has taken over some oil fields in the South part of Libya with possibly around 6,000 soldiers. After our initial two-week surge, we might just move over to Libya and take care of the 6,000 XTREM members there. Of course, Madam President, this would be done only with your approval."

The General finished explaining that Joint Chiefs had put this plan together. "This represents a vigorous timetable of 14 days. It would require careful satellite monitoring in every sector with pinpoint accuracy for air and naval strikes when called in. The timetable would not allow the XTREM forces to regroup to attack one area or another as they would be attacked in a 360-degree circle. Mobil detention centers for those surrendering are established and staffed by non-special military forces from each country in the coalition. We are ready as soon as we get the go-ahead from your office Madame President, to hold video conferences with all coalition military leaders to finalize plans."

Stan was amazed at the planning the Joint Chiefs had done but was surprised that a name for this mission was not used. He commented, "General – I really appreciate how thorough the Joint Chiefs plan is, but I was wondering if you had a name for this mission?" Not wanting to open this door up for discussion, Stan quickly said, "I think it should be called Freedom 41. Freedom has many meanings for all countries, and Montana was the 41st state in our union."

The President jumped in with, "I like that, Dr. Pace. Let's not quibble over a name for the mission, Freedom 41 it is. I will get started with the Secretary of State contacting the countries on your list General and will get back to you as soon as possible. Anything else?" No one spoke. With that, everyone stood up as the President did, and after she left the room with the Director of National Intelligence, the rest of the group left as well.

As Stan walked out of the Situation Room, part of him wished he was still in uniform as an Army Ranger and would be part of Freedom 41. But, that quickly vanished when he thought of everything that had to be cranked up at the CDC. We were ripe for another chemical attack in a form that we might not have considered. The deaths in Freedom, MT gave the idiots and copycats ideas that could be used on a smaller scale than Steven and Darcy concocted.

Chapter 32 – Washington D.C. / Freedom, MT

Stan was anxious to get back with the FBI to hear any further information regarding their investigations in Chicago and California. Everything they had shared previously had been confirmed, and the threat, in their opinion, was confined to ricin attacks on all Catholic Churches on Catholic World Peace Day. No other attacks of this nature were imminent. The Press Secretary would be holding a press conference outlining what the FBI had reported.

When he got back to his hotel room, he called Dr. Cindy Robinson in Freedom, MT, as he had told her he would give her a call when things had settled down.

"Hello, Dr. Robinson, Dr. Stan Pace here. Just wanted to give you a call to see how you were doing?"

"Please call me Cindy, Dr. Pace," she replied.

"And please call me Stan, Cindy," he agreed. "So, how are you, and how are things in Freedom?"

"Well, I am getting by. I saw the President's address to the nation, and I thought it was terrific. She is a strong leader." Cindy paused for a bit and continued, "Many of the people that died were not only former patients but were friends of mine and leaders in our community. So, from that perspective, it will take me and our small city a long time to recover from this attack. We lost 153 men, women, and children representing about 50 or so households. Since most of these residents are homegrown, it would be a stretch to think that the homes that are now vacant will find new tenants anytime soon. The businesses that are in Freedom may find that they cannot be sustained with this loss. The public school is also facing a funding problem with the loss of so many children. I am rambling, aren't I?"

Stan hadn't thought about everything that Cindy was sharing, but as a small town with this type of disaster, the city itself might just cease to exist in time. The silence on his end actually startled him, "Sorry for the silence Cindy. I was just letting what you said sink in. So, are you taking care of yourself? It is easy to focus on everyone else, but you have to make sure you are taking care of yourself."

She paused for a while and said, "I know you are right, Stan, and I guess I just haven't had time to process everything in such a short time. My parents are coming in next week. That will be great, and maybe then I can start dealing with everything. But, on the other hand, I have to ask myself if it is wise for me to stay here. It was only going to be a stop in my growth as a physician. But if I leave, who would stay and help?"

"Cindy," he responded anxiously, "There is a lot to think through, and I'm sure your parents can help you. I'm glad you are ok. If after things settle down and you would like to get out of town and come to Atlanta for a visit, you would be welcome." He hesitated to share any more as he found Cindy Robinson to be very interesting amid everything in his short stay in Freedom. During that tragedy was not the time to get to know her better, but it was something on his mind. We just sort of hit it off.

"I just might take you up on that, Stan," Cindy said in a bright tone." Give me some time, and I will get back to you." She thought he was charming, influential, and might be fun to be around in a normal situation.

"Fine, Cindy," Stan commented. "I would look forward to your visit. I thought we had some chemistry in our brief discussions. Take care and call if you need anything," and he hung up. He had been so busy in his professional life that he had put his social life on the back burner. His relationship with the President probably needed to stay totally professional now in the wake of everything that had taken place. She didn't need a scandal to derail her from her critical tasks ahead. He now needed some rest.

Sister Deb had shared with Dr. Robinson that Father John's brother, Jason, and his fiancé had decided to get married by a justice of the peace with family only present, and then instead of going on a honeymoon, they would come to Freedom for ten days to help where they could. Jason said to Sister Deb, "I know that is what John would want."

Chapter 33 – The White House

The next day President Sutton and the Secretary of Staff were on video conference calls all morning reviewing with the heads of states about the ricin attack, how it was avoided and what could have happened. After much discussion, all eight countries agreed that the killing and potential threats to everyone in the world were a reality. No government wanted to wait until a terrorist attack, like the one that partially succeeded, but the master plan failed in the USA took place in their country. The saying "What did you know and when did you know it" was shared as a common theme and one that no country's leadership could survive if something happened with the knowledge that they possessed.

The Russians were already in Syria trying to protect the current administration and were bombing questionable targets with US forces present. They agreed to halt those operations until Freedom 41 was completed.

The special forces teams in all eight countries were always ready and trained. Representatives from each special force with the Joint Chiefs were designated to do the actual detailed planning on a secure video conference that afternoon. The President called Dr. Pace and requested that he attend this meeting if any questions would come up regarding chemical attacks that the Joint Chiefs could not answer. "Dr. Pace, I need you to be part of this planning as I trust your judgment and need a person there that is not just interested in just war games."

Stan was surprised as well as excited to help and said, "I am honored, Madam President, and I will take part in whatever you deem necessary." With that, they hung up, and he hurried over to the White House for the afternoon meeting.

The meeting started promptly at 2:00 p.m. EST. on a secure video conference. First on the agenda was what actual satellite help to identify targets that would be available from each country that had this technology. The USA, Russia, Great Britain, and Turkey volunteered their total help in this area. A subcommittee from these countries would quickly survey the entire area XTREM claimed to control. Using the very best technology the world had to offer made this task easier than anticipated.

Since the USA already had Navy vessels close at hand, the other countries saw no need to mobilize other ships.

Uniforms were agreed upon. They would be desert camouflage for all special forces so that XTREM could not identify what countries the soldiers represented. The only markings would be a patch that said Freedom 41 International Force, with the Earth in the background.

Rules of Engagement (ROE) for all allied forces were discussed. It was agreed that the basics of the Sanremo Handbook on Rules of Engagement would direct the allies even though not every special forces group could guarantee that their missions would adhere perfectly to the ROE. The significant difficulties the forces would come against were identifying friendlies to XTREM and nonfriendlies. When in doubt, the wellbeing of the forces would be paramount. This would be beyond the scope of the ROE Handbook.

General Else looked over to me and said, "The President has asked you to be present in the command post when Freedom 41 begins. Your responsibilities will be only to observe and give feedback to the President during the campaign. Are we clear on this, Dr. Pace?"

"Of course," he answered. "I am honored to be a part of the campaign and will help in any way you see fit." He thanked me and continued with the planning. Stan was sure his presence was not his first choice, but he had no choice since the President had given him an order.

Sunday, November 5st was targeted for codeword Jump Start/Freedom 41 as airdrops to all 5 of the insertion points would take place at 0800 Eastern European Time (EET). All satellites were coordinated, a command center was established in Turkey, and all Navy Ships, Air and Drone support would be ready. The airdrop would include the special forces and from various countries – main battle tanks, infantry fighting vehicles, armored personnel carriers, mine-protected vehicles, light armored vehicles, light utility vehicles, fuel trucks, combat engineering vehicles, self-propelled artillery, anti-aircraft, unmanned vehicles, and some very top-secret experimental vehicles. There was enough ammunition, water, and supplies to last the special forces14 days easily in the drop. Generals from each country and Dr. Stan Pace observing would coordinate via satellite operations from Turkey at the central command.

The meeting concluded at 4:00 P.M. EST, and General Else and Stan went to the Oval Office to brief the President. General Else reviewed all aspects of the campaign. When he finished, he said, "Madam President – this campaign will go down in history as one of the greatest short-term campaigns by allied forces against a force that has no sense of the value of human life. The attack on Freedom and the potential to kill up to 79 million Catholics in the United States made the leaders in almost every country in the world very troubled."

He continued, "The general theme by the military leaders in our allied forces was that if this could happen in the USA – it could happen anywhere and with XTREM targeting all Christians in the world, killing them, beheading them, burning them – all ages – raping women, etc. – a coalition similar to that in WWII really needed to be considered. The rest world could see the potential for XTREM to spread their warped sense of humanity. In WWII, the Allies promoted the alliance to stop German, Japanese, and Italian aggression. France, Poland, and Great Britain were soon joined by the British Commonwealth and later the USA. But this type of monster, XTREM, is different than Hitler in that our world is different, and you cannot always identify your enemy, such as in the Freedom attack. The XTREM ideology must not appear to anyone to be exciting or courageous."

"General Else," the President commented, "I thank you for your fine work in the Freedom 41 preparations. After this meeting, I will brief both Homeland Security and House and Senate Committees. Also – a special thanks to you, Dr.

Pace, for your hard work with the FBI and CDC, bringing to closure all aspects of the Freedom, MT attack."

The President continued, "This is a very nervous time for the Country, my office, our military, and the World. A plan of this nature has not taken place since WWII. The major difference in our operation is the technology available in today's world compared to that in the 1940s," she concluded her remarks. She explained that on November 5, 2017, she would coordinate a worldwide address with all the allied country's heads of state to be delivered in unison, describing Jump Start/Freedom 41 as it would be happening.

All the planning and preparations for Operation Freedom 41 were in place.

Chapter 34 – St. Patrick's Church, Cumming, Iowa

St. Patrick's Catholic Church is a small, rural Madison County, Iowa church. The church is surrounded by 20 acres, including timber, grassland, cultivated fields, and the parish cemetery, where many of the first parishioners were laid to rest. The community was settled in the early 1850s by Irish immigrants. It gained international attention when Pope John Paul II visited the church in 1979. (Wikipedia)

Father Francis Bean had been the priest for the past fifteen years, was retired, and due to a stroke, was deaf but still could speak clearly and read lips. Due to the severe shortage of priests, the dioceses had permitted him to continue to serve St. Patrick's.

When the authorities came to the church to collect the lethal incense on September 23rd, Father Bean gave them a bag he had prepared, knowing they were coming. But, being very forgetful, he knew that he needed to gather all of them up before he forgot to or misplaced them.

Over the years, Father Bean had relished in the different kinds and smells of incense and had a private collection in his office that he used sparingly. When the Pope proclaimed that special green incense would be used on September 24th, he ordered two sticks and placed one in his private collection and the other in the cabinet with the rest of the incense. Being very forgetful, Father Bean did not remember to give the authorities the one he placed in his private collection.

On Sunday, October 8th, Father Bean went to his collection, selected an exquisite green stick wrapped in plastic, and placed it in the thurible to be used at the only Sunday service at 10:30 a.m. As usual, he greeted the small congregation at the door, and then, a few minutes before the service started, he put on his garments, stepped onto the altar, and started the Mass.

When the Peace Be with You portion of the Mass approached, he went to the thurible, opened the small glass door, lit the incense stick, began the back and forth motion around the altar, and then moved toward the congregation.

James O'Neal, seated in the front pew, had read everything about the Freedom tragedy, and the color green startled him. The color was never used before and was why the Pope had ordered it to be used only on the Catholic Peace celebration on September 24th. He shouted in a panicked voice, "Everyone get out of the church NOW. The incense is green!"

Father Bean never heard the screaming but did see the entire congregation running toward the entrance. He set the thurible down and wondered what was wrong. That was the last Mass he would ever perform.

When Dr. Stan Pace heard about the incident in Cumming, Iowa, he had one terrible thought, "Did we really get all the green incense sticks?"

Epilogue

Freedom 41 was a huge success. Within two weeks, XTREM had all but been eradicated, but their ideology remained. Few surrendered as was predicted. Occupied territories held by XTREM or close to being held were returned to their original status. After the initial invasion, 10,000 of the special forces also went into Libya and reclaimed the XTREM occupied oil fields.

The destruction of irreplaceable historical artwork, buildings, and ancient relics could never be replaced, which, along with the needless deaths of innocent men, women, and children, would haunt the region and world forever. Many mass graves were found in areas outside of villages. Local residents who had survived were thankful for the allied troops removing the terrible XTREM influences.

While there would be some that would continue their XTREM beliefs, as groups, their power would be minimal. The fear of radicalized homegrown terrorist threats would remain like what happened in Freedom, MT, and other places in the World. The USA Federal agencies tasked with preventing terrorist efforts would continue to be vigorous in their efforts to stop such attacks.

Professor Pace was asked to retire and remain on emeritus status by UCB. He was unhappy about this forced retirement, but UCB could not support him after his name was associated with Steven Habid and Darcy Oban. The politics were just too much for the university to deal with, especially in recruiting future students. Rather than contesting this forced retirement, Professor Pace just packed up his office and went home. He was offered many speaking engagements as a renowned bio-chem professor that had experienced a tragic situation. In his third speaking engagement, he died of a massive heart attack, having never recovered from the shame caused by his two prize students.

Steven Habid had pleaded guilty, and because of his help in making the entire plan public as well as implicating Darcy, he would spend the rest of his life in ADX Florence, Colorado, a high-security prison in solitary confinement except an hour alone daily in the yard.

In Al Bukamal, Syria, a Navy Seal Sniper named Andy Vich, from a small town in Montana, sat on top of a building with his spotter next to him. Their satellite and local intel had indicated that Darcy Oban was in a small ground-floor apartment in Al Bukamal. Multiple sources confirmed this. As an Army Ranger retired, Dr. Stan Pace had requested to accompany Andy on this mission as he had lost his father over her actions and watched over 150 die in Montana. They had waited all afternoon for Darcy Habid to come out from her apartment with her boyfriend, Aazim. Aazim was not his target. Andy knew that neither of them usually surfaced in the daylight.

Knowing this, Stan could not resist going to their front door of the small apartment, knocking, and when Aazim answered, saying, "Is Darcy here?" Aazim quickly turned as Darcy came to the door, and she lost all the color in her face as she recognized Professor Pace's son from CNN coverage.

Stan said, "Hi Darcy – I am not in any official capacity as I have no authority in this country. You know who I am. I just wanted you to know that it was easy to find you, and at some point, you will pay for all the people who died in Montana as well as causing the death of my father, who so believed in you. Unlike all the people in Montana that perished, I'm sure you will die a quick and painless death and one I hope someday to witness." With that, Stan turned and walked down the street, turned behind a building, and joined Andy Vich and his spotter on the roof. Aazim watched him carefully walk away until he turned the corner and quickly called his father.

Andy's idol was the American Sniper Chris Kyle. Like Chris, Andy used a Remington 700 long action rifle with a Lilia precision barrel, a McMillian A-2 tactical stock, a Remington factory trigger, an M16 extractor bolt modification, a Nightforce NXS 8-332x56 scope, and a Knights Armament MK-11 Suppressor. His accuracy was perfect at 800 meters, and he was only 300 meters from the front door of his target's dwelling.

The weather was perfect – very little wind and mild temperatures for this region. Fifteen minutes after sunset, Darcy Habid and her boyfriend, Aazim, exited the dwelling, each carrying a small suitcase spooked no doubt by Stan Pace's visit. Andy's spotter was now shooting pictures with his very portable camera and confirmed the target. Andy adjusted his sights and breathed as per his extensive sniper training and experience, keeping his heart rate around 52 beats per minute, considered optimal. He centered his cross-hairs on his target's head and gently squeezed the trigger. Darcy's head exploded from a silent shot, and she dropped backward, dead before she hit the ground. The spotter had filmed everything for military confirmation. Andy said a short silent prayer as he always did after a kill and rolled to his left, and they both quickly began packing up. Stan could not help crying as he saw his father's face as he closed his eyes. So much pain – so much sorrow – it just seemed never to end. His PTSD was in total control.

Aazim fell to the ground on his knees and looked at Darcy, and saw that she was gone. Since he was still alive, he knew he was not a target of the sniper. Aazim scrambled back into the dwelling, leaving the door open, and looked out into the dimness at Darcy, laying on the ground. His rage was mounting by the minute. He vowed to avenge Darcy's death and said to himself, "I will attack America in a way they do not expect and bring them to their knees. Allah Akbar."